"How's the tour going?" David asked.

"Daddy, come help us carry Christmas decorations," his daughter Reba said. "We're going to help Jenny decorate the house."

"Sounds like fun," David responded after a hesitation so brief Jenny thought that someone would have to know him very well to even notice it was there.

And, despite all the time and distance, she still knew him.

She knew what the season ahead would be like for him, the constant inner battle between providing a happy experience for his daughters and—might as well be honest about it— having as little as possible to do with her. She sensed her own conflict about that. She could understand all too well why he would feel the way he did, but this was her home.

"Jenny, how come you're wrinkling up your forehead like that?" Rowe asked, while Reba crinkled her own forehead in concern.

"I was just thinking that we have a lot of boxes to carry," Jenny said hurriedly. "So it's a good thing your dad is going to help us out."

Donna Gartshore loves reading and writing. She also writes short stories, poetry and devotionals. She often veers off to the book section in the grocery store when she should be buying food. Besides talking about books and writing, Donna loves spending time with her daughter, Sunday family suppers and engaging online with the writing community.

Books by Donna Gartshore

Love Inspired

Instant Family
Instant Father
Finding Her Voice
Finding Their Christmas Home

Visit the Author Profile page at LoveInspired.com.

Finding Their Christmas Home

Donna Gartshore

LOVE INSPIRED
INSPIRATIONAL ROMANCE

LOVE INSPIRED®
INSPIRATIONAL ROMANCE

ISBN-13: 978-1-335-59694-9

Finding Their Christmas Home

Recycling programs
for this product may
not exist in your area.

Love Inspired
22 Adelaide St. West, 41st Floor
Toronto, Ontario M5H 4E3, Canada
www.LoveInspired.com

Printed in U.S.A.

It is of the Lord's mercies that we are not consumed, because his compassions fail not. They are new every morning: great is thy faithfulness.
—*Lamentations* 3:22–23

For my daughter, my mom, my sissies and my extended family. I thank God for all of you.

Also, to the Saskatchewan writing community: you continually amaze and humble me with your talent, your diversity and your encouragement. I am honored to be among you.

Thank you to Tamela, Melissa and the whole Love Inspired team. I could not do this alone!

Chapter One

Dear Lord, this cannot be happening, not after everything.

David Hart slowly opened his eyes, which he'd closed momentarily, not so much for his quick prayer but in the hope that the woman in front of him would be gone when he looked again.

But, no, Jenny Powell still stood in front of him, and even though it had been fifteen years since he'd seen her—since she'd abruptly left town after the cancer she'd fought had gone into remission—he would have known her anywhere.

But what was she doing here—now—at her grandmother, Estelle Winter's house in Living Skies, Saskatchewan? The house known as Christmas House, because of its decorations and warm, welcoming atmosphere during the Christmas season, had always held a place of honor.

At five foot eleven, she could almost meet him eye to eye, which she was doing now, in fact, with an expression that was as chagrined and befuddled as his must be. She was still slim but muscular, her face still long, narrow and firm-jawed, lit by eyes as blue as a Saskatchewan-summer sky. She still smelled like she was perpetually baking doughnuts, a sweet comforting scent that had always made him want to reach out to her.

An odd thing to remember when faced with someone he had never wanted to see again.

"Awkward," Rowena, one of his eight-year-old twins stage-whispered. Beside her, Reba giggled, a sound that lifted his heart with gratitude. Eighteen months ago, he hadn't known if he would ever hear that sound again.

But their reactions brought attention to the fact that he and Jenny must be gaping at each other like fish wondering who was going to be the next to get caught.

Well, it wasn't going to be him.

"Girls, this is someone I used to know way back in high school," David said hurriedly, as Jenny led them into the house, trying to sound as if he was introducing them to a mere acquaintance. "This is Jenny—is it still Powell?"

There was a beat while she recovered herself, yanking her eyes away from his face to sweep over the twins before returning them to his face.

"Yes."

So, she had never married. Or she had and was now divorced, like he was. He thought about the way he had foolishly believed that life was good. But then Reba's cancer diagnosis had happened, and three months later his wife, Cheryl, had walked out the door.

Due to Reba's recovery and Rowena's own struggles with being the twin of a cancer survivor, David had obtained permission for the girls to start their Christmas vacation early, and he'd taken time off from work to spend more time with them. Their best friends' families had headed to warmer climates this holiday season, and he knew the girls would be at loose ends. But now the only thing his heart anticipated was more trouble ahead, and having Jenny Powell show up after all these years did nothing to counteract that feeling.

"So…twins?" Jenny focused on the girls again who were studying her with unabashed curiosity. For once Reba wasn't fidgeting with her growing-out hair, too mesmerized, David supposed, by the pretty stranger that had come to the door.

The spacious, four-story house had always been decorated to the hilt, and visitors were welcome from two to six every afternoon but Sunday to admire the decorations, socialize and enjoy Christmas cookies and refreshments.

This year David sometimes wondered if Estelle even knew that it was Christmas.

Now he wondered what Estelle thought about Jenny being home and why she hadn't said anything to prepare him.

But he supposed it was enough that she had offered him and his daughters a place to stay while their own home underwent repairs needed for water damage caused by a burst pipe.

At first he wasn't keen on the idea. They could have easily stayed at a hotel, or at his parents' house, although the thought of that made him grimace. Finally he had accepted her offer, but only after Estelle had agreed to let him help with the upkeep at the house.

"I like your hair," Reba said wistfully, her fingers finding her pixie-cut length hair after all, as she looked at Jenny's shiny, shoulder-length waves. David had always loved her chestnut hair, with just a hint of auburn.

It had always reminded him of those autumn days long ago when their whole lives were ahead of them and rich with possibilities.

"How'd you know we were twins?" Rowena asked. "A lot of people don't get that."

"Because you're taller and have darker hair and your eyes aren't the same color, right?" Jenny said sagely.

Rowe nodded, her eyes, brown like his, snapped with energy, while Reba's blue eyes had a softer light.

"Maybe I'm just a really good guesser," Jenny said teasingly. "Or maybe—" she hesitated and her gaze flickered over David's face "—I heard about you two from my grandmother. But," she added, looking from one to the other, "you *do* have the same noses, and you stand the same way, and your voices are similar. Yours," she pointed at Reba, "is just a little softer."

David didn't know what rattled him more, the way Jenny was instantly bonding with his daughters or the fact that she knew things about his life when he knew virtually nothing about hers.

Residual anger surged through him and David breathed in and out slowly and flexed his fingers open and closed.

"Where is your grandmother, by the way?" he asked. "You obviously weren't expecting me. Didn't Estelle say anything?"

"She's taking a nap," Jenny said. "And as a matter of fact, no, she didn't tell me, although I'm sure she meant to." She tried to smile, but it didn't quite reach her eyes. "What are you doing here?"

"A pipe burst in our house," David said by way of brief explanation, not that he owed her one. But the way Jenny nodded and didn't ask why he wasn't staying at his own parents' home or in a hotel conveyed that she still understood more about him than he wanted her to.

The four of them now grouped in the living room but, still on edge, remained standing.

"Is she… How do you think Estelle's doing?" He didn't want to think about whether Jenny Powell still knew him or not.

Or about why she had come home after all these years.

By the way she worked her jaw and reached up to tuck her hair behind her ears, David could tell she wasn't sure how much she wanted to open up to him either. "She's, um, definitely gotten older."

"Bor-ing," Rowena announced clearly before faking an exaggerated coughing fit. "Can we see our rooms, puh-lease?"

"Rowena, please don't be rude." David's voice rushed out in an exasperated sigh. The family counselor in him tried to remember that it wasn't at all easy to be the sibling, especially the twin, of someone who was ill. It was all too easy for the healthy one to get lost in the merry-go-round of appointments and treatments.

But as a father left to raise two girls on his own, he couldn't let the behavior slide.

"Sorry," she mumbled.

"Rowena…" Jenny said slowly as recognition dawned on her face.

"Sometimes people call me Rowe," the girl interjected.

"And Rebecca?" she said, smiling at Reba.

"Yes," Reba said softly.

Jenny looked back at David with a thoughtful smile. *"Ivanhoe."*

"Their mother just liked the names," he answered abruptly. There was absolutely no way that he was going down memory lane with her.

One summer, when Jenny and David were about thirteen years old, her grandpa had said that if they'd let him read *Ivanhoe* to them every evening for half an hour after supper, he would give them money to buy as many magazines or comics as they wanted at the end of the summer. It turned them both on to a love of the classics, and they'd never looked back.

At least he hadn't—he wouldn't presume anything about Jenny at this point.

But he couldn't help wondering if she still loved the classics, if she still liked to write stories and what stories she had found on her travels throughout Canada and the United States

He averted his eyes from her gaze, picking up his luggage. "If you can show us to our rooms…"

Jenny blinked away what may have been a glimmer of hurt, but he didn't care.

He didn't.

"Of course," she said. "And when Gran wakes up I'll let her know you're here. There should be shortbread and gingersnaps and some fruit in the kitchen if you're hungry."

Jenny continued to chat about the availability of food and drink as they went up a flight of stairs.

There was suddenly nothing David wanted more than to be away from that voice, that face, that sugar and apple smell, everything that mocked him for believing he'd gotten over her.

"Great, thanks," he said, cutting her off when they

stopped in front of the room that was his for however long his home repairs took.

"Okay," Jenny said hesitantly, "And the girls will be right across the hall."

"I don't get my own room?" Rowena asked in dismay. "I do at home, and this house is a lot bigger than ours."

"Rowe!" David snapped, the end of his rope unraveling quickly.

"I just thought you might like to be together," Jenny said, twirling a strand of hair around her finger which meant that she doubted herself.

Rowena rolled her eyes scornfully.

"Jenny, thank you for everything, but we need a moment here," David said. It boggled him to even think that he would be sleeping under the same roof as Jenny, but he was sure she would want to keep her distance as much as he did.

After she departed, the rush of relief he experienced from the reprieve of sharing the same space with her trumped his frustration with Rowe.

"Just put your suitcases in the room," he told them. "We'll take a look around and figure out the sleeping arrangements later."

"I don't mind sharing with you, Rowe," Reba said. She had always been the one who had never been a fighter—until her cancer came along. David secretly wondered if Rowena's constant provocations had been the push that Reba had needed.

As they walked through the house, David wondered if it would be possible to give his daughters the Christmas House experience that he remembered from his youth. He remembered the glorious smell of fresh sugar cookies and gingerbread, the scents of mint and chocolate that wafted out as soon as the door to Christmas House opened.

Today there had been nothing remotely like that.

The decorations were meager at best: a tired-looking garland wound around the banister, and a few silver and gold baubles were placed in a glass bowl on a table in the hallway. But what really concerned him were the obvious signs that the house needed some serious upgrades.

It had taken some doing to convince the girls that staying at a neighbor's house would be even more fun than staying at a hotel, which might have at least offered them a pool for entertainment.

Christmas House wasn't exactly living up to the promises he'd made, but he still tried to hold fast to the idea that it could be healing for all of them.

Lord, if You have any ideas here, I'd sure appreciate You letting me know.

He doubted Jenny was going to stick around long enough to see whether her grandmother's house would be fully restored or not, and it didn't look like Estelle would be able to manage the house much longer on her own.

An idea dawned.

He would help Estelle fix things up, as he'd promised. But he would also let her know that when she was ready to sell, he would make sure he was ready to buy. There would be room for his counseling practice here, and it would be a fresh start for him and the girls.

She won't stay, he told himself, pushing away the picture of Jenny's surprised face, the look in her eyes when she realized what the twins' names were. *She won't care.*

He was tired of having so many regrets. It was time for a future full of hope.

Jenny made it down the hallway with steady steps, but the second she turned the corner out of their eyesight, she exhaled and began to tremble.

Dear God, I didn't know that was going to be so hard... Her attempted prayer ping-ponged around her head.

As if it wasn't enough that she had drained her bank account traveling and that she'd neglected to take any significant steps toward her goal of being a writer—a goal she'd held since discovering the challenging but rewarding experience of putting her thoughts into words for school essays and the school's newspaper and yearbook—now she was faced with sharing the same roof with an ex she'd done an exceedingly bad job of breaking up with.

Of course she had known that if she ever came back to Living Skies she would see David Hart. Several mutual friends sent her updates on his life, letting her know when he got married and when the twins were born.

Did anyone realize or care that it broke her heart?

But that's on you, she scolded herself as she had so often done before. But she still believed in the decision she'd made, in the life she had chosen.

When her cancer diagnosis had upended her carefree high-school existence, she knew that whatever happened she would never be the same again. And when she was given the gift of remission, she knew that she would never be content if she didn't find out what the rest of the world had to offer outside the comfortable boundaries of Living Skies, Saskatchewan.

But that didn't mean that the love she'd had for David Hart wasn't real. The love that had grown from the childish affection for the boy next door who was always there when she needed him to the gradual realization that their friendship had turned into something much deeper.

"Bess? Are you there?"

Gran was awake and calling for Jenny's mother. Jenny shoved down her anxiety, reminding herself that Gran was often at her most confused when she was just waking up. She would have to remind her again that her parents were serving with a church-missionary team in Peru and, as they often did, were letting another missionary couple stay at their house while they were gone.

It wasn't her parents, in fact, who'd alerted her to the decline in Gran but rather her good friend, Grace Severight, a practical-minded physical therapist whom she had known since high school.

Jenny tapped softly on the door to her room and went inside. "It's me, Gran. Jenny."

Gran was sitting up in bed, propped up against the garish pink satin slip-covered pillows she adored, her eyes focused, if a bit sleepy still.

"Oh, Jenny," she said calmly. "Have the guests arrived?"

"Yes," Jenny answered, then couldn't help adding. "Gran, you could have told me it was going to be David."

"I'm sure I did…" Gran shifted position restlessly, her eyes clouded with confusion. "I meant to."

"It's okay," Jenny said hurriedly to reassure her grandmother. "You probably did tell me, and I just forgot."

Gran nodded and leaned back onto her pillows.

How Jenny had loved this house, and especially this

bedroom, while she was growing up. It had been the guest room, but after Gramps had passed away, Gran declared that it was too lonely staying in their room without him and proceeded to turn the guest room into her personal haven. Jenny's parents were practical people, determined to live on less themselves so that they would have more to give to others. Jenny respected their choices, but she loved feeling like a princess whenever she entered Gran's room, where her grandmother gave in to her love of pastel colors, frills and lace, and a collection of Dresden china dolls.

Jenny's nose involuntarily crinkled as she took in the musty smell of the room. Dust was actually visible on the surfaces of the dresser and end tables. The house simply didn't have the life and joy it used to and instead signaled Gran's failing health.

"Was it good for you to see David again?" Gran asked, but before Jenny could think about how she could possibly answer that question, she added, "Shame about his little girl, isn't it?"

"A shame about what?" Jenny asked, but the answer hit her as soon as the question was out of her mouth. Reba's shorn hair, the look in her eyes that was too old for an eight-year-old. She'd seen that look in her own mirror: cancer.

She wondered why no one had thought to pass that bit of news on but maybe, knowing her own medical history, they'd decided to draw the line there.

She was swallowed in sorrow for what David had been through and was no doubt still going through. She silently sent up a prayer that God pay special attention to him and his daughters.

Jenny turned her full attention to Gran.

"Did you have a good nap?"

Gran sniffed haughtily. "I was just resting my eyes. It's not like I have time to nap with this house and guests to look after."

That sounded like the Gran Jenny knew, and she grinned with relief. Oh, how she loved this feisty woman, whose hair had been a cloud of white as long as she could remember. With her curls and her dimpling smile, Gran reminded Jenny of an octogenarian Shirley Temple. She loved to sing and dance while she was doing housework. Or at least, she used to. She had done everything she could to make her house a haven for a lonely little girl.

Jenny knew that bringing God's word to people wherever they could was important to her parents, but that often meant they were away from home, and because of school and her activities, Jenny wasn't always able to go with them. If it hadn't been for the steady, comforting and encouraging presence of Gran, she didn't know what she would have done.

She was reassured by her grandmother's words, taking them as evidence that she was still herself. Of course, Gran was getting older and it was a big house, so it was only natural that some of the upkeep would slide. But that didn't mean that Gran herself wasn't just fine.

"Do you remember David Hart?" Gran asked brightly. "Did I tell you that he's bringing his twins here for Christmas? One of them had cancer, poor little tyke."

Jenny's stomach sank like a lead balloon at Gran's words.

"Yes, I saw David and the girls," she answered, not knowing what else to say. "I greeted them at the door and showed them to their rooms."

"I wonder why I didn't do that," Gran murmured, her eyes clouded with confusion. "I guess I am feeling a little tired."

Jenny leaned forward and hugged her grandmother, swallowing her anxiety.

"You go ahead and rest as much as you need to, Gran. I'll go and see if they're getting settled in."

She would have to stay positive and not let her concern make Gran even more anxious, even though playing host to David and his girls caused her already-clenching stomach to curdle in apprehension. She couldn't imagine David would be too pleased with it either.

After reassuring Gran again that it was good for her to keep resting, Jenny went downstairs and found David in the kitchen sitting on one of the red vinyl chairs at the table. He was alone, and his head was bowed. She wondered for a moment if he was praying and didn't want to intrude, but then he lifted his head and looked at her.

"I was just wondering how many hours we spent doing homework and talking at this table," he said.

Jenny started to smile, but David's face went stony as if he immediately regretted the words.

"The girls are unpacking," he said.

"That's good." Jenny swallowed, unsure of what to say next.

"So you must be thinking this is pretty strange, us being here," David said.

One thing was certain: he was still blunt, preferring to get to the heart of matters. So much about him was still the same. There was no doubt that he was older, but his brown eyes were still dark and expressive, his face was still square and his complexion olive, his shoulders still broad. But the weariness etched on his face and in the slight slope of his shoulders indicated that the past several years had not been easy ones.

Suddenly she realized she was staring and averted her eyes. Silence hovered between them.

"Gran didn't tell me you were coming," Jenny finally broke the silence. "The house isn't…it isn't the same, is it?"

David's face softened into something like an apology. "I did tell Estelle I want to help her fix things up. I haven't kept in touch with her as much as I should, what with Reba getting sick and… You've heard Reba had cancer? It's in remission now."

"I just heard. I'm so sorry."

"Thank you. So are you going to sit down or just stand there?"

Yes, he really was as blunt as ever. Despite the tension between them, Jenny fought a grin as she lowered herself into the chair across from him. She'd consider it a blessing if they got to be on civil terms, never mind friendly ones.

David leaned back in his chair and surveyed the surrounding kitchen. Jenny's surge of amusement subsided as she tried to see the space through his eyes.

Gran's fondness for bright, warm colors was still apparent in the hues of red and yellow, but the paint was chipping, and instead of the intoxicating smells of Christmas baking that would usually fill the kitchen at this time of year, it had the same musty smell as Gran's bedroom.

"Is Estelle thinking about selling?" David asked. "It looks like the upkeep of the place is getting to be more than she can handle. I'll do what I can while I'm here, but I'm not a professional contractor by any means."

Jenny's territorial reaction was visceral and immediate. She didn't want Gran to sell the house. Somewhere deep inside, even though she didn't know if or when she'd ever come back to Living Skies, she always counted on this house as being a safe place for her to land, a place that she needed now more than ever.

She had been fired from her most recent job working for a home-renovations contractor in Burnaby, British Columbia. The reason her boss gave was *insubordination*, but she knew it was because she'd refused to lie to the clients on his behalf. She'd thought about fighting it, but then Grace's phone call had come about Gran, and it seemed like the perfect time to come home.

"Gran doesn't plan to sell," Jenny told David firmly. "As a matter of fact, now that I'm home, I plan to help her fix the house up and stay here to make sure she's looked after, so there's really no need for your help."

"You're staying?" David's eyebrows rose in accompaniment to his incredulous tone.

Jenny began to give a sharp retort, but then Gran appeared in the kitchen doorway. She was dressed in a lilac sweater and a gray skirt but still wore her bedroom slippers.

"Hi, kids," she said cheerfully, as if it was only yesterday that David and Jenny had sat at her kitchen table together. "Can I get you a snack?"

Jenny swallowed a pit of anxiety. But even more hurtful than Gran's confusion was the cold look on David's face that said he'd slammed the door on those memories.

Chapter Two

"No, thank you, Estelle," David answered politely, his jaw tightening with the effort, while he fumed inwardly at Jenny's words. He didn't believe for a second that she planned to stay in town. He also didn't appreciate her reacting like he was some unscrupulous developer about to evict her grandmother from her home. He only wanted the best for Estelle, but when she was no longer able to remain in her house, he would offer her a fair price and would do everything he could to honor its traditions.

A long-suppressed memory rushed through his mind like a tidal wave. When he and Jenny were dating in high school, he had often thought about marrying her and living in this house with her. And when Gran and Gramps got too old to get the house ready for the holidays, they would take over the legacy and be the ones who brought joy to others.

When Jenny became ill, he'd wanted to protect her and pray for her healing, making sure he was with her every step of the way. He hadn't told anyone, not even her, but the house had become a beacon of hope for him, helping him to believe, in the worst moments of Jenny's cancer, that there was hope and that they would have a future together.

Why, God? Why did You let me believe so fully in something that was destined to fail? It was a question he had asked so many times. He no longer expected an answer, but the question still had sharp teeth that sunk in deep and wouldn't let go.

Jenny had approached her grandmother and was murmuring something to her, a gentle hand on her arm.

Then he heard Rowe's voice and her loud footsteps before she appeared in the kitchen. He couldn't help welcoming the distraction. Rowe had always known how to make an entrance. Reba followed closely behind.

"We're bored," Rowena announced.

In that moment, David fervently wished that a broken pipe wasn't keeping him from grabbing that as an excuse to go home right then and there.

"Well, you wouldn't be bored if you really knew this house," Jenny spoke up, darting a glance at him. She urged Gran to take a seat at the table and poured her a glass of orange juice.

"We've been here before," Rowe said.

"Ah, but you've just been here to eat some of Gran's cookies and see the Christmas decorations. You've never had an actual tour of the house with someone who knows all of its secrets."

"Secrets?" Reba's eyes grew large. "Like secret passages and stuff?" There was nothing more enticing for a girl who loved to read books that featured hidden rooms and secret gardens.

Jenny had always known how to connect with people, but David wasn't about to let his girls get attached to someone who could be gone again before they knew it.

He was about to offer his daughters another distraction when his cell phone rang. The screen told him that it was the owner of the building, where he'd leased his office space for the past few years, who was chomping at the bit to sell the building and take an early retirement, which meant that David was under pressure to find new office space.

David let the call go to voice mail. Couldn't he at least get through the holidays without having to think about this? But he knew that his landlord would keep at David until he got what he wanted. Last time they spoke, he'd said that it was because David had been such a good tenant all these years that he was allowing him time to find a place to relocate his office before selling the building. But, with every day that passed, David could tell that long cracks were running through that patience, like ice breaking away from the middle of a thinly frozen lake.

He looked between Jenny and his girls and decided he would let them take her up on her offer—just this once—so that he could return the phone call and ask for just a bit more time, just until the New Year. Surely, God would help him find a solution by then.

"If you wouldn't mind keeping the girls occupied for few minutes," he said, not quite meeting Jenny's eyes, "I'd appreciate that."

"I'd be happy to," Jenny answered. "We'll start in the attic and work our way down."

"Didn't there used to be a lot more lights and stuff?" Reba asked thoughtfully.

"Maybe you and Rowe can help me fix this place up," Jenny suggested. "Do you like to bake?"

The girls nodded, and Rowena allowed her carefully placed mask of perpetual detachment to slip.

"Can we do hairstyles too?" she asked, studying Jenny's pretty hair.

Shorn Reba bit her lip, her thin shoulders slumping.

David's heart flipped in his chest. A vision of high-school Jenny flashed into this mind: bald, proud and defiant, and still so beautiful.

"How about we do manicures instead?" Jenny said, the slightest tremor threaded through her voice. "I'm pretty good at nail art, if I do say so."

She sent him a questioning look, and David gratefully nodded.

Jenny had hurt him, but the evidence that there was good in her was abundant in Reba's eyes shining their own gratitude.

"Can you sit with Gran while she finishes her juice?" Jenny asked.

"Of course," David said. "I have to return a phone call, but I'll be right here with her."

"Oh, my," Gran said suddenly. "Stop talking about me like I'm not here. I'm not an infant."

"I'm sorry, Gran, I know you're not," Jenny said to reassure her. "I just thought you might enjoy the company."

"Estelle, will you excuse me while I make one phone call?" David asked, after Jenny and the twins had departed to find the house's secrets.

Gran gave a go-ahead wave that reminded him of the British royal family.

He punched in the number, and Leo Adderson answered after half a ring.

"Been trying to reach you," he said, dismissing any formalities.

David could picture the man he'd known since he was the high-school football team coach, his athletic bulk turned to paunchiness, and a pen making its twirling way in and out of his thick fingers.

"I know you need to finalize things, Leo," David said, "but the girls and I—" He stopped himself. He promised himself and God that he would never use Reba's illness to manipulate any situation. Instead he said, "We're getting into the holiday season, and it's tough to get things done. I can't move my office without a space to move to. We've also had a burst pipe at the house," he added, just in case that made any difference to Leo.

It didn't.

"But it's totally a buyer's market out there, Dave," Leo reminded him for the umpteenth time.

"I know, Leo. I'll have something in place early in the New Year," David assured him, once again praying that it would be true.

"Yeah, I guess that's okay," Leo said. "But you know I'd really like to get this wrapped up. If I don't hear from you by, say, January 5, I'll give you another call."

I'm sure you will, David thought as he ended the call.

"You've got some trouble, don't you?" Gran's eyes shone over her juice glass, scrutinizing yet somehow guileless like a child's eyes, "Well, never you mind." She patted his hand reassuringly. "Jenny's home now, and the two of you will figure it out.

David had no intention of letting Jenny be part of the solution but he still wished he could catch some of Gran's confidence.

* * *

It was only after they'd started to climb the winding stairs to the attic that Jenny wondered what kind of shape it would be in. She couldn't imagine the last time Gran would have gone up there, and maybe it wasn't safe for the girls. But she heard them chattering excitedly behind her and didn't want to disappoint them.

Besides, she needed the breathing room from their dad. There was something going on with him, no doubt about it. Something beyond an ex-wife, a recovering daughter and another one determined to keep a firm grip on her share of the attention in whatever way she could. She had always been able to sense when things were off-kilter with David, and it was rather unnerving to discover that, after all these years, she still could.

"How are you two doing on the stairs?" she asked over her shoulder, being careful not to single Reba out. Thankfully, her own cancer had stayed in remission, but the memory of debilitating exhaustion lingered.

Both girls said they were good. Then they rounded the last corner, and Jenny cautiously edged open the door.

The attic looked and even smelled exactly the way she remembered, and she blinked back unexpected tears.

The scent memories came from the pinewood paneling, the old books—*The Bobbsey Twins*, *Donna Parker*, *Nancy Drew* and others—stacked on the bookshelves, the *National Geographic* magazines piled into wicker baskets. The smell of mothballs wafted from the large brown wardrobe, where dresses, coats and suits hung with memories of good times clinging to them.

Jenny could picture herself, plain as day, sitting

cross-legged on the floor, flipping through those magazines and books.

Often David had been with her too...

"What are these?" Rowena spotted a shelf that housed a variety of old toys and games and headed toward them. "I'm too old for these kind of toys," she quickly clarified, as she picked up a jack-in-the-box and jiggled the turning crank a little. "I just find old stuff educational."

"Of course," Jenny smiled.

"You said there are secret places?" Reba asked.

"There are. I could show you one right now," Jenny said. "That is," she added, glancing at Rowe, "if you don't think you're too old for it."

"I guess it might be fun," Rowena said, trying to sound casual, though anticipation gleamed in her eyes, dark like her father's.

Jenny led them into the small attic bathroom, and like she'd done it an hour ago instead of several years, she slid out a panel from the back of the wall and said, "If you squeeze through here and just follow the little passageway, you'll find a window that opens up onto the roof. Your dad and I used to sit out there sometimes—"

She stopped herself, knowing that David wouldn't want her discussing their past relationship with his girls.

But the twins were too busy poking their heads through the opening to pay any attention to what she was saying.

"Can we go out there?" Rowena asked.

"Please?" Reba added.

"It's winter," Jenny reminded them. "It's cold, and the roof is probably icy."

"We could put on our coats and stuff," Rowena persisted.

"We'll have to ask your dad," Jenny said, without much hope that the answer would be yes, for more than one reason. "But, if you want to walk the passageway and then come back, I can wait here."

"That's not fun," Rowe protested, but Reba said she wanted to, so Rowe shrugged her shoulders and followed.

When they got back from their short excursion, Jenny said, "I know that Gran used to keep boxes of Christmas decorations up here. Do you want to see if we can find some and you can help me decorate the house?"

It didn't take them long to unearth the boxes and they were just beginning to organize them to carry downstairs when they heard David's voice.

"How's the tour going?" he called out.

"Daddy, come help us carry Christmas decorations," Reba said. "We're going to help Jenny decorate the house."

"Sounds like that might be fun," David responded after a hesitation so brief that Jenny thought that someone would have to know him very well to even know it was there.

Despite all the time and distance, she still knew him.

She knew what the Christmas season would be like for him, the constant inner battle between providing a happy time for his daughters and—might as well be honest about it—having as little as possible to do with her. She was having her own conflict about that. She could understand all too well why he would feel the way he did, but this was her home, and she wasn't going to let him make her feel like a stranger here.

"Jenny, how come you're wrinkling up your forehead

like that?" Rowe asked, while Reba crinkled her own forehead in concern.

"I was just thinking that we have a lot of boxes to carry," Jenny said hurriedly. "So it's a good thing your dad is going to help us out."

David reached the attic just as she was saying it, and Jenny wondered if he too would be slammed with the immediacy of memories. She was grateful for the insistent chatter and pointing from the twins as they instructed him what ornaments they wanted to use.

"Was Gran okay when you left her?" Jenny asked when the twins were in another corner, stacking boxes.

Uncertainty flittered through David's brown eyes. "I think so."

"Why did you come up here if you weren't sure?" Jenny didn't want to raise her voice and draw the twins' attention, but her tone was taut like the tightening of an out-of-tune violin string.

"She was fine," David clarified. "She just seems a bit confused about..." He suddenly looked like the shy boy who had confessed on a memorable summer night that his feelings for her had gone beyond friendship. "She seems confused about us."

"Ready to go, Dad?" Rowe cut in before Jenny could ask him for more details. Just as well. She had a pretty good idea what he meant, and there was no reason to force another awkward conversation.

After a couple of trips, they had the boxes carried downstairs and into the living room. Jenny invited Gran to sit in her favorite chair to take part in the unpacking and have a say in what decorations she wanted up. All the while, a persistent worry gnawed at her stomach. Although her grandmother seemed happy enough to participate now, she'd done nothing on her own to get the house ready for Christmas.

The biting in her gut cut deeper as Jenny wondered how in the world she would manage to decorate the house, bake cookies and plan her future—whatever that meant—with an ex-boyfriend and his twin daughters living in the house too.

"Are you okay, Jen?" David asked. "Your color isn't great," he said, in his blunt David way.

From her time as a natural class leader through the various careers she'd sampled in her years of travel, Jenny made sure to always project an aura of confidence. Not even Gran had been able to pinpoint when anxiety was about to collapse the facade like David could.

"I'm okay." She made herself breathe slowly in and out. "I'm just realizing there's a lot to do."

"This house is too much for Estelle," David said, "and for you."

So that was it. Jenny exhaled slowly and squared her shoulders. He didn't really care about her, not anymore.

Being unjustly dismissed from her last job had tainted her openhearted view of the world. It was no longer easy to believe that people were always good at heart.

Or that God was still guiding her path.

"Reba, Rowe, show me what you've found." She spoke perhaps a bit more loudly than was necessary and with an extra sprinkle of cheerful confidence. "You know, if I think hard I can remember exactly what this room looked like when I was your age. Would you like to help me recreate it?"

For the next hour or so, with Gran supervising from

her chair, and while David handed over boxes and reached the high places yet remained conspicuously quiet, Jenny and the twins brought some Christmas spirit back into the living room.

It was only one room but it was a start.

Jenny stepped back and took in the Nativity scene arranged in its place of honor on the coffee table, the green garland draped across the fireplace mantel, the gold and silver baubles in glass bowls on end tables. It all looked wonderful, but something was missing.

"My angels!" Gran exclaimed. "My angels need to go right there." She pointed at the curio cabinet in the corner.

Jenny had fond memories of arranging and rearranging Gran's collection of angels. It had been one of her favorite parts of Christmas. How could she have forgotten that?

"I'll go find them," she said quickly. "Be right back."

She sprinted off and was halfway up the attic stairs again when a board splintered suddenly, and her foot slipped through and caught between the broken pieces.

She cried out, and it seemed only seconds before David was on the steps behind her.

"Easy," he said, coaxing her to balance on him while he leaned over her foot and gently, ever so gently, maneuvered it out. "I've got you."

I've got you. Words David had spoken to her in sweeter times that were long gone.

Her ankle throbbed like crazy but still ached less than her heart.

Chapter Three

"What happened?" Rowena asked, her eyes glinting sharply, as David came back into the room with Jenny hobbling beside him, her arm draped around his shoulder.

Reba watched them too, her soft blue eyes puzzled, her fingers nervously flicking at her pixie cut

David knew his daughters were angry and hurt by their mother leaving them. But even though they claimed they didn't want to see her, that didn't mean they wanted to see him with anyone else.

Dear Lord, please let me know right now if we should just go to a hotel, after all.

They hadn't even spent their first night here, and he'd already had about as much as he could take. It didn't help matters to have Jenny in such close proximity that her sugary-cinnamon scent conjured memories of much better times.

He rather unceremoniously deposited her into the nearest chair. "I'll get some ice." He had to get away, if even for a moment, to give himself some breathing room.

"One of the attic stairs broke," he heard Jenny explain while he looked for something to put the ice in. "Gran, we'll have to get those fixed. Have you noticed problems with any of the other steps?"

David's conscience jabbed. Despite everything going on, he had to keep his promise to Estelle to do some repairs.

"I don't really get up that way anymore," Gran said as David brought an ice pack into the living room.

Well, that explained why the house wasn't decorated, among other things.

"You won't be going back up there either," he told his daughters. "Not until I have a chance to thoroughly check things out."

"It's not yours to check out," Jenny reminded him.

He didn't answer as he retrieved a footstool and lifted her foot up on it. She winced, and he made himself ignore the empathetic pain that shot through him.

He still couldn't stand to see her hurt in any way.

"I don't think it's broken," he said, prodding gently at it. "But it's badly bruised. Can you move it at all?"

Jenny grimaced as she slowly rotated her ankle. She gasped a bit, then gritted her teeth and tried it again.

She had always been a fighter.

He arranged the ice pack across her foot and stood up.

"I know it's not mine to fix, but as I mentioned, I told your Gran that I would help her with some things around the house, and that's what I intend to do. Someone needs to go through this place from top to bottom and make a list of everything that needs to be done."

"I hope you're not thinking it's going to be up for sale," Jenny said, "because it's not."

"I don't think that's your decision to make," David

said. "But at this point I'm really just offering to help. If you care for your grandmother, and I know that you do, wouldn't it be good to know that her house was a safe place for her to live?"

"That's not fair," Jenny grumbled, and he almost wanted to smile—almost.

She tilted her head and studied him through narrowed eyes. "Since when do you know anything about home repairs? You're still a family counselor, aren't you?"

So somehow she had kept tabs on what he'd been doing since they'd broken up. That fact did make him smile inside.

"I am," he agreed, "but unless you've forgotten who my father is, you'll know that I grew up learning a thing or two."

His father, Ivan Hart, owned Hart's Hardware on Main Street and had, in fact, wanted David, his only son, to follow him into the family business. He wasn't shy about letting David know he didn't think his career as a counselor was an appropriate one for a real man, as he put it, just one of a few reasons why it wasn't easy to stay with his parents at his childhood home.

"Of course I remember your father," Jenny said, wistfully. "How are your parents doing?"

"They're both doing well. Thanks for asking. I imagine you'll run into them at some point if you plan on staying in town for a while."

He would never tell her that his mother cried all those years ago, when he'd told her that Jenny had broken up with him and left town.

"And how are your parents?" he asked, knowing it was the polite thing to do.

"They're away on another mission," Jenny said.

"So their house is...?" He realized he hadn't thought to wonder why she was staying with Estelle, maybe because it had been such a common occurrence in the past.

"There's another missionary couple staying there, and I think some international students too."

"I see."

He would never disrespect Jenny's parents, but it seemed just like them to offer their home to others without stopping to consider the needs of their own daughter.

Jenny lifted her chin. "I think Gran should have a say in what happens here. After all, it is her house."

Rowe and Reba had pulled chairs up beside Gran and were exclaiming over some sparkly, multicolored ornaments.

"They just don't make them like they used to," Gran said. "Everything comes out of a factory these days, and it all looks the same. Such silly things people put on their trees too. Cartoon characters, action figures." She frowned and looked over at Jenny. "Where are my angels?"

"I didn't have a chance to get them, Gran," Jenny explained again. "I hurt my foot going up the attic stairs."

"I'll go find them right away," David promised. He crossed the room to where the older woman sat. He crouched beside her chair and took her hand. "Estelle, Jenny already hurt herself on a broken stair, and we don't want that to happen to you too. Remember, you and I agreed that I was going to help you with some house repairs?"

Out of the corner of his eye, he could see Jenny shifting in her chair, but she remained quiet.

Estelle patted his hand and beamed fondly at him. "You're a good boy, David Hart. You always were." She turned back to the girls and the ornaments. "But isn't this your vacation?" She wrinkled her forehead, trying to remember all the details.

"Some vacation." David was about to speak to Rowena when he realized that the exasperated outburst had come from Reba.

She was right, of course.

Dear Lord, what am I doing here? I convinced my girls to give this a try, and already there's so much getting in the way. What are we supposed to do?

"Maybe it could be both?" Jenny asked.

David stood up and turned to look at Jenny. That was the last thing he expected to hear from her.

But, then again, when had Jenny Powell ever done what he expected?

Are You sure this is what You want me to do, Lord?

In her life, and particularly on her travels, Jenny had learned to count on God's guidance, to listen for His voice in her heart, but often He surprised her.

Take right now, for example. He couldn't really be asking her to risk her tenuous grasp on a place to call home for the sake of a man who had never forgiven her and likely never would.

But still, the inner voice prodded her, there was Gran to consider, the house was falling into disrepair, and now she had her throbbing ankle to prove that it was deteriorating and that the maintenance was more than she and her grandmother could handle by themselves.

She didn't want to view David as a rival. She trusted him, despite not having seen him for years, by her own choice she reminded herself. She did believe that first and foremost he cared about Gran and didn't want her living in an unsafe environment.

She considered the twins and how, somehow, she could see things in both of them that reminded her of herself. Rowe's take-charge attitude, which she suspected hid a fear that she would never be enough. In Reba, she saw the girl who'd never wanted to be any trouble, especially not for her parents who did so much for others. She'd actually felt guilty when her cancer diagnosis made them cancel one of their mission trips.

David had been with her then, every step of the way.

She knew it could not have been easy for Reba to articulate her frustration.

Yes, there was no doubt about it, God was definitely telling her something.

"Since you and Gran had an agreement," she said, before she could change her mind, "you can help her with the repairs around the house, and if you agree, I'd like to make sure that Rowe and Reba have a good time while they're here."

"Manicures," Rowena reminded her. "You said we could do manicures."

"You're right, I did say that."

"I like pink polish the best," Reba said with shy pleasure.

"I don't know if…" David began, then stopped.

But it wasn't hard for Jenny to figure out what he'd been about to say. Clearly he wasn't keen on his daughters spending too much time with her—the woman who had broken his heart. But, if he had a better solution, she wished he would offer it.

Besides, didn't he realize that she'd broken her own heart too?

"You won't be much fun if you can't walk," David finally said.

Jenny carefully rotated her ankle, praying the worst of the pain was gone. It had subsided considerably, though it still ached.

David was watching her closely. "I'll get some more ice," he said.

"Dad, you're the one who talked us into coming here," Rowe reminded him.

"I did." He nodded. "Okay, I think we've got a deal."

"Should we shake on it?" Jenny jibed, as gratitude and sorrow swirled through her. David was still taking care of her, but that was just the kind of person he was. Always the first to welcome newcomers to their school or church, eager to help someone carry a heavy bag of groceries to their car, and especially the kind of guy who'd stand by a terrified high-school girl with cancer and promise to never leave.

No, she had left him instead, and she knew that his gentle ministrations with her ankle right now didn't mean that he had forgiven her. He would have helped anyone in the same situation.

She sat up straighter, pulling her foot away from David's hand. "I think I'm ready to try standing up now," she declared.

"Are you sure?" he asked. "I think it's too soon."

Ignoring him she stood, wobbled, clamped her eyes shut against a dizzying wave of pain, steadied herself and stayed standing. She couldn't stop herself from flashing a triumphant look in his direction but couldn't read his expression in response, except that if she didn't know better, she might have thought he was proud of her.

She would keep up her end of the deal and do what she could to ensure that the twins enjoyed their stay.

But if David Hart thought that helping with repairs gave him any claim on this house, or that she or Gran were going anywhere, now or in the future, he had better think again.

Chapter Four

Surreal was the only way that Jenny could think to describe the feeling of walking down Main Street. It was like being in a time warp, except for a few small changes, to convince herself that she wasn't just dreaming about being back in town.

She had done that often enough.

But, in her dreams, everything was the same. She and David were young again, together and happy and there was no cancer.

In an odd way, she was almost grateful for the lingering twinge of pain in her ankle, since it kept her grounded in the reality of her present circumstances.

Although Jenny knew the word must be out that she was back in Living Skies, she had been staying close to home to avoid the questions that were sure to come when she ran into others. But, after enduring an uncomfortable evening and a restless night, she decided that anything that gave her some space from David Hart was a good idea. She'd eagerly volunteered to get some groceries, including the ingredients that were needed for the cookie-baking she'd promised Rowe and Reba.

The thought of Reba made her breath catch a little. The young girl was definitely not a complainer, but Jenny could see how she would suddenly slam up against walls of debilitating fatigue. She remembered well the struggle and frustration of wanting to do everything, only to have her body betray her. She wanted both girls to have a wonderful holiday season at Christmas House and to share with them all the activities associated with a Christmas there. But she knew she would have to constantly gauge how Reba was feeling.

David would expect no less of her.

David.

She could find as many excuses as possible to physically keep her distance, but she couldn't escape the thoughts in her head. None of her dreams or daydreams—some pleasant, others nerve-racking—came remotely close to preparing her for what it was like to see David Hart in person again.

Like the town of Living Skies itself, there was enough familiar about him to cause the kind of melancholy ache she got when hearing a song she thought she'd long forgotten until one note would cause a flood of memories to come pouring back.

He was still tall and slender, but not lanky as he had been growing up. There was something more solid about him now. He still had those deep brown eyes, so earnest and beseeching that, unless you knew him well, you'd fail to see the mischief in them.

Growing up, she'd been the outgoing, boisterous one, always popular, always the center of things. She'd played on the athletic teams, performed in the school musicals and was a leader. David was much quieter, more studious. When Gran and their friends at school said *opposites attract*, she knew that they had people like her and David in mind. What they didn't know was the sense of humor that lurked beneath the surface, and that he was, more often than not, the instigator behind their escapades.

Jenny's smile was tinged with sadness as she remembered a time she'd believed, with no question, that he would always be part of her life.

Soon, though, a different nostalgia swept over her as she went through the door of Graham's Grocers and was immediately greeted with the fresh, earthy and citrusy smells of the produce aisle, mingled with the scents of bouquets of arranged flowers.

Added to that were wafts of pine and peppermint, the sparkle of multicolored lights strung from the ceiling and wrapped around wooden beam posts in the store, along with yards of garland in gold and silver, red and green.

"Jenny Powell! Well, unless you can convince me that I'm dreaming, you've just made my entire day. No, forget that, you've made my whole year."

"Mrs. Graham! Are you getting younger instead of older? Or do my eyes deceive me?"

Jenny didn't know how she was able to so easily slip back into the kind of banter she had always had with the plump, twinkling-eyed woman before her. All she knew was that she was overwhelmingly happy to see Fern Graham again.

"Oh, never mind your teasing, you. Come give me a hug."

"Who said I was teasing?" Jenny said as she eagerly bent down to receive one of Fern's famous hugs.

For a moment, Jenny was six years old again and back in Fern Graham's Sunday-school class.

Fern gave her another squeeze, then released her and stepped back, studying Jenny with open scrutiny.

"You're still a beauty, no doubt about that," Fern declared, but the compliment was marred by a slight frown. "But you're too thin, and you look tired. Have you been taking care of yourself?"

"I think I'm probably just a little out of sorts from travel," Jenny hedged, not wanting to get into the emotional storm that was stirred first by seeing the state of the house and Gran's confusion, and then blown into a huge gust-up by having David there.

"How did Wilson's surgery go?" she asked, taking the focus off her but also genuinely interested to hear about Fern's outwardly tough but inwardly sweet husband. "I heard he had knee-replacement surgery."

"Oh, the surgery went fine, but he's been an absolute grouch," Fern said placidly. "He can't stand being away from the store, and he thinks it's too much to handle on my own."

"Is it?" Jenny asked tentatively. Was this the Lord opening a door for her? She was going to need to find some kind employment sooner rather than later, especially if Gran needed her to stay.

Correction: Gran did need her to stay, she just wasn't likely to admit it. Jenny never had to look far to see where she got her own stubbornness from.

"Oh, there are never enough hours in the day for everything," Fern said, "But that's to be expected. I give the Holy Spirit full credit for giving me the time and energy to get the place decorated for Christmas. Aside from that, I serve the customers and keep the cash balanced, and frankly, that's enough for me right now. No one but me needs to know what a mess the storage room is. Oops," she clapped her hand over her mouth, her brown eyes dancing merrily above it. "And I guess now you know too."

"I could help you with that," Jenny said, not allowing time to talk herself out of making the offer. "I could help with whatever you needed. If I'm going to stay and help Gran, I'm going to need a job."

There it was. Her next breath was a silent but hopeful prayer.

Now Fern's eyes were thoughtful. She ran her slender fingers through her graying hair.

"Are you really planning to stay?" she asked.

Impatience shot through Jenny like a flare but was quickly doused as she acknowledged that it was only fair for Fern to ask. She'd known Fern Graham her whole life, and while the woman was friendly and always talkative, she didn't gossip or say anything thoughtlessly.

"That's a fair question," Jenny said. "I know I haven't been home for years but…"

The bell on the door signaled another customer, and she braced herself wondering who it was and what their reaction would be to seeing her. She was relieved when it was someone she didn't recognize.

"Good morning Claire." Fern smiled at an extremely pretty plus-sized woman. "It'll just take me a second here to get your coffee and muffin. I got a little distracted here visiting with an old friend—I should say a long-time friend," she corrected herself. "Claire, this is Jenny Powell, she's come home to visit her grandmother. Jenny, this is Claire Casey. She runs the flower shop."

The women exchanged greetings and shook hands.

"Claire does wonderful things with her flower arrangements," Fern said.

"Oh, thank you, I love bringing a little bit of beauty and happiness to people's lives when I can." Claire's warm green eyes sparkled, showing the enthusiasm she felt for her work.

Fern handed Claire her coffee in a recyclable cup along with a small brown paper bag.

Claire lifted the bag in a little salute. "The best gluten-free blueberry muffin in town," she said. "I see extra miles in spin class in my future. It was nice meeting you, Jenny. I'm sure I'll be seeing you around."

After Claire had left, Jenny said, "She seems lovely."

"She is," Fern agreed. "When the little Hart girl was in the hospital, she sent flowers every day, fun and girly bouquets to make her smile."

Fern stopped speaking, her eyes scanning Jenny's face for her reaction.

"Just so you know, there's nothing between David and Claire," she explained. "Claire is just a thoughtful person, and she would have done the same for anyone."

"It's perfectly fine even if there is something between them," Jenny said, her neutral tone contradicted by her clenching stomach.

"Are you sure?" Fern asked, furrowing her brow and tilting her head. "Because I always thought that you and David Hart would end up together. I couldn't stop feeling that way even after he'd married someone else. If you were to ask me, I think he still—"

"It's been great chatting, Fern," Jenny interjected hastily. "But I really came in to get some baking ingredients, and I don't want to keep Gran waiting."

If there was anything she wanted to hear even less than that David was in love with someone else, it was that he was still in love with her.

Because that would mean she had to face her own feelings.

"I don't suppose you've run into David yet?" Fern asked.

Jenny was tempted to ignore the question, but she wanted to be truthful with Fern, who was bound to find out anyway where David was staying.

"He—um—he and his girls are staying at Christmas House. There was a burst pipe at his place, and I guess he thought it would be more fun for the girls than staying at a hotel."

Fern nodded. "David's father never makes it easy on him, does he?" Then added, "I didn't realize that Estelle had opened Christmas House."

Instead of answering, Jenny asked, "Fern, how does my grandma seem to you?"

Sympathy poured into Fern's eyes, and the struggle on her face showed that she was torn between being encouraging and being honest.

"Well, she's always got a great attitude, but I'd have to say that the house is getting to be too much for her. So you've come home at just the right time."

Jenny tasted the tang of guilt.

"Does she seem forgetful to you?" she asked.

"Well…yes, but I think we all get a little forgetful now and then," Fern said.

Jenny gave Fern's arm a little squeeze. "I know you're just trying to stop me from worrying too much," she said. "But I can see myself how much things have changed with Gran."

Fern nodded sadly. "I guess there's no stopping the march of time. All we can do is try our best to be there for the people who need us."

"And now you sound like the Sunday-school teacher I remember," Jenny said fondly. "Now, come help me pick out some ingredients before things get too busy in here."

As they ambled up the baking aisle, Fern said, "So you and David Hart are living in the same house?"

Jenny grimaced slightly. "Yes, and no matter how awkward you imagine it is, it barely scratches the surface."

Fern chuckled softly. "I wonder…" she began, then stopped herself.

"What do you wonder?" Jenny asked, although she was already afraid that she knew the answer.

Fern picked up a bag of butterscotch chips and another of chocolate chips and offered them both to Jenny.

Jenny selected the chocolate, hardly thinking about it, still waiting for Fern's answer.

"Well, they do say that God works in mysterious ways."

Jenny shook her head. "No way, not a chance."

So why did her heart quicken and her cheeks flush at the thought of a second chance with David Hart?

"He'll have some decisions to make if his landlord manages to sell the building where David's office is located," Fern commented.

Jenny almost asked for more details but then stopped herself. That would explain his sudden interest in Christmas House. If it ever went up for sale there would be plenty of room there to live and for office space too.

She straightened her spine and began to briskly select the rest of the baking goods she needed.

She couldn't afford to worry about David or the girls, not when she had so much at stake in her own life.

The sounds of chatter and laughter coming from the kitchen didn't comfort David. Instead, they only seemed to enhance the temporary respite from his real life. Not that it was much of a reprieve anyway, not with Jenny home and bringing memories to the surface that he had fought so hard to dismiss from his mind.

He could hear Rowe's raucous laugh and Reba's softer giggle, and while he was grateful for both, his gratitude was dampened by wishing that he could be the one making them happy. Or, more to the point, he wished they were bonding with anyone but Jenny.

This was ridiculous. He couldn't spend his day hovering like an interloper outside the kitchen, even if the smells of chocolate, peppermint and cinnamon were tempting enough to make him linger. Estelle was napping, and his girls were happy. Now would be the perfect time to wander through the house and make a list of the repairs he could take care of.

He'd nailed a board over the broken attic step. Jenny's slight limp when she came into the kitchen the next morning to grab a piece of toast and a cup of coffee had stabbed at him more than he'd anticipated. He reminded himself that she was more than capable of taking care of herself and had done so for many years.

Dear Lord, You know the struggle I went through to come to any kind of peace after she left. I'm asking You, please, to let me keep that peace. I can't go through it all again.

David quietly turned from the kitchen and headed

toward the stairs to the second floor, where he and the girls were staying.

As a child, he'd thought that Christmas House was a mansion. When he was older, he realized that it was simply a large, older home, but compared to the three-bedroom bungalow he had grown up in, the house still had a sense of spaciousness and possibility that he'd never experienced in his childhood home. Now, the door also seemed closed to possibilities in the home he shared with his girls.

More than the size, though, it was the security and welcome he always felt there, something he didn't always have growing up in a house where he was constantly peppered with reminders that he wasn't doing the things his parents expected him to do.

When David graduated from university with honors and eventually opened his own counseling practice, his father had subtly scorned his choice of career.

"Seems to me that people should be able to solve their own problems," he would grumble, "not expect someone else to make sense of their lives for them."

David shook the thought away, reminding himself that he loved and respected his parents, and even though they didn't often see eye to eye, they had stepped up and offered their support when Reba got her cancer diagnosis, and then when Cheryl had left. He would do what he could to make sure he sustained a relationship with his mother and father because Rowe and Reba needed family, now more than ever.

But he hadn't told them about the burst pipe or about where they were staying. He could virtually hear his father's voice hammering at the nonsense of staying at a neighbor's house, and maybe the real problem was

David still wasn't quite sure about his own decision—especially when Christmas House wasn't exactly living up to its name.

One thing was sure: he didn't want Jenny to be the only reason his girls had a good time here. He wasn't going to let them believe she was someone they could count on.

When he reached the top of the stairs, he decided he might as well start in his bedroom. The guest room was tidy, with a pale yellow chenille bedspread, white curtains and hardwood floors with a gold and maroon flowered area rug. But there was now something a bit dreary about it.

He walked around it, testing dresser drawers, quietly opened and closed the bedroom door a few times. Everything seemed to be fine; the room just needed a thorough dusting and some fresh paint.

Next, he went into the balcony room where Rowe and Reba were staying. Usually, the girls—Rowe, in any case—liked having their own space, but the charm of the little room, with a screened-in door leading out to a little balcony that was close enough to an apple tree to smell its fresh blossoms and enticing fruit, had made them agree to share.

Rowe's suitcase was on the floor, her clothes spilling out of it, while Reba had hers neatly folded and on the shelf in the small closet. She had always been an organized child, but with the cancer she had become even more so, as if worried about being more trouble than the disease relentlessly caused, through no fault of her own.

The thought of it shattered David.

It wasn't balcony weather, but he suddenly needed fresh air.

The door was stubborn, so David gave it a good yank. It gave a wrenching screech, and he stumbled backward a few steps as the screen door came loose.

Unfortunately, the noise carried, and only seconds later he could hear footsteps hurrying up the stairs, Jenny followed by his daughters. He groaned inwardly as he prepared himself for the barrage of questions. But, really, there was no way to explain standing in the middle of a room with a balcony door in his hand except by the truth.

"Daaad, you broke our door!" Rowena wailed, while Reba's eyes didn't know whether to dance with laughter or fill with tears.

Eventually, laughter won out, and soon Rowe joined in. The sound of his daughters' mingled giggles almost made the mishap worthwhile.

Estelle had come out from her room sleepy and befuddled, and Jenny went over to her.

"Come on, Gran," she said, still looking at David. "I'll get you settled in the parlor with some tea." The next words were directed at him. "I'll be back to find out what happened up here. Girls," she said and her tone gentled, "can you please go back to the kitchen and call me when the timer dings? We'll ice the cookies after they've cooled."

To his surprise, Jenny was back moments later, and Estelle was still with her, eyes snapping with indignation.

"David," she fumed, "will you please tell this granddaughter of mine that I am not an infant and I'm perfectly capable of deciding what happens to this house, which still is, may I add, *my* home."

So Jenny must have told her grandmother that she was afraid he wanted to buy her house.

"I'm not ready to move yet, so don't push me," Estelle said firmly, sounding strong and sure, like she'd never had a minute of confusion in her life. "But when I do move, the house goes to Jenny. That's a given. She's my granddaughter, and she'll need a place to stay."

It took every ounce of willpower and a quick, pleading prayer for David not to point out that Living Skies hadn't been Jenny's home for years and there was no reason to believe she was back for good.

"I don't see what all the fuss is about, anyway," Jenny's grandmother grumbled. "Whether I leave the house to you," she said as she pointed at Jenny, "or sell it to you," she pointed at David, "my plan always was that you'd both be living here after you're married."

David was blindsided by Estelle's assumption that nothing had changed between him and Jenny. It was like the years had never passed and nothing had changed. He didn't know what was worse, realizing how confused Estelle really was or knowing how irrevocably things had changed.

Chapter Five

Jenny wondered if the shocked expression on David's face mirrored her own. She guessed that it did, which was almost funny, but she couldn't quite get there.

But it served as yet another reminder that Gran simply wasn't herself, making her even more determined to stay in Living Skies and make sure that the woman who had always looked out for her would be cared for herself.

Before either she or David could correct Gran, she heard the timer on the oven go off, giving Jenny an excuse to hurry down the stairs and into the kitchen where she almost ran smack-dab into the girls who were running out to call for her.

"The cookies smell delicious," Reba said, breathless with excitement. At least, Jenny hoped it was just that. She anxiously scanned the girl's face, checking her pallor and for any signs of fatigue. Yes, Reba was in remission, but Jenny knew better than most how important it was to monitor any symptoms.

Maybe if her parents had paid more attention to her early signs… But, no, she and the Lord had walked that road of resentment and eventual acceptance, and there was no point in backsliding into that pointless pit again.

Then she noticed that David was studying his daughter with the same concern. Not an anxiety that anyone who didn't know him well would spot, or that would alarm Reba—he would always be careful not to do that. But she saw it in the tightening of his jaw and the slight squinting of his left eye. And it unsettled her that, after so many years, she could still read him.

But she couldn't deny being happy that David was a parent who paid attention. Besides, if his focus stayed on Reba, maybe they could skirt past that awkward and oh-so-wrong assumption of Gran's.

Speaking of Gran, she'd made her way down to the kitchen as well, grinning with the same kind of joyful anticipation as the twins as she jostled her way in between them to help lift the tray of cookies out of the oven.

Jenny flew in their direction, fearful of a mishap. Gran wasn't even wearing oven mitts.

"Let me do that," she said, trying to quell the edge of panic in her voice. She prayed for patience. Gran couldn't help it, she reminded herself, which was exactly the reason she was here.

Out of the corner of her eye, she was aware that David was subtly trying to draw Reba aside to talk to her, but her body language showed that she was assuring him she was fine. Trying not to exhale in relief, Jenny grabbed the oven mitts, which were close by on the counter, and deftly slid the cookie tray out of the oven.

"Careful, it's very hot," she warned.

"Stop acting like I've never been in my own kitchen or cooked a thing in my life," Gran snapped, sounding more like herself again. Somehow, that only made Jenny's emotions more jumbled.

She heard David cautioning his daughters that the cookies would have to cool before they could start decorating them.

Reba said wistfully, "Remember how Mom always used to say that we should eat the burned or broken cookies first so they didn't feel left out?"

Rowena's face hardened with a mild disdain.

Jenny held her breath. Obviously there were going to be some bitter feelings, but did that have to mean that a young girl wasn't allowed to remember some of the good things about her mother? Then an expression crossed David's face like he was reminding himself of the same thing, and he said, "That's right, she did used to say that, didn't she? Well, no sense ruining a good tradition." He grinned and snatched up a cookie, holding it by the corner and blowing on it. Giggling, his daughters followed suit.

Thank you for the reminder, Lord, Jenny prayed. It was all too easy to imagine the sadness and resentment that must permeate their home. For the first time since she'd laid eyes on David again, she allowed herself to let down her guard.

David had brought his daughters here in the hopes of giving them all a break from what they'd been going through. Spending time in this house with Gran had soothed Jenny's bruised heart on many occasions. She couldn't bear the thought of doing less than what she knew Gran—and God—would expect from her. She had to let Christmas House do what it did best and that meant helping to encourage all the love, joy and hope that the Lord brought to their lives.

Her heart jolted like a skate hitting a bumpy patch of ice on a frozen pond. She hoped that God would help her efforts even if her emotions didn't always match.

Sometimes when Jenny was out of sorts, Gran would tell her to smile even when she didn't feel like it. "It's okay to fake it till you make it," she would say.

So now she fixed a smile on David and the girls and said, "Are those cookies cooled off yet? I can't wait to start decorating them. What about you?"

She started taking out the icing and multi-colored sprinkles she had bought to decorate the cookies. Soon, Rowe and Reba crowded in beside her at the counter, chatting and suggesting festive designs that could be made with the icing

When they went with armfuls of bags to the table, David took the opportunity to sidle up beside her and murmur, "So that's it, then?"

"Is what it?" She blinked and slid her eyes away, but she'd never been particularly good at being evasive, especially not with someone who knew her as well as David did.

"Jenny, I know you have a huge problem with me being here, and even more so with the thought of me purchasing this house from your grandmother. I can't believe we're just going to decorate the cookies and pretend that everything is okay. I know you better than that."

His latter words caused something caught in that strange land between a laugh and sob to rumble through her. She disguised her emotions by clearing her throat, then went on the defensive, planting her hands on her hips, only having to tilt her chin up slightly for her eyes to meet his.

"Correct me if I'm wrong," she said in a tone she

managed to make piercing, although she kept the volume under her breath, "but didn't you come here to give Rowe and Reba a lovely Christmas?"

David lowered his shoulders and exhaled softly.

"You're right," he said.

"Could you repeat that?" Jenny couldn't resist. But he didn't smile, so she shrugged and turned away.

"Jenny, wait a second."

She turned back, slightly wary.

"I'm still me," he said.

"Okay…"

He made a frustrated gesture with his hands. "What I'm trying to say is that even though we haven't seen each other in years, we did used to trust each other. I think we still could."

Jenny listened because she realized, as David spoke, that maybe she didn't trust him after all, not just because he might want Gran's house but because even though she was the one who'd left, she didn't trust him because he had let her go.

She doesn't trust me.

Jenny had always had the most expressive eyes, no matter how hard she tried to quell her reactions.

David remembered suddenly that he used to mock brag about his uncanny powers of insight when he foresaw her next move in a chess game or to choose the exact movie she wanted to see before she had a chance to tell him. But the truth was that he had always been able to read her. Even now, when he hadn't seen her in so many years, her face still easily gave up her secrets, like turning to the last page of a mystery novel to see how it ends.

His skin prickled with the sting of that realization.

She thought he was here to steal her grandmother's house right out from under her. If she would just sit down with him and be reasonable for a few minutes, he could help her see the positive aspects in the situation. She would have to admit that her grandmother's days of being able to stay in the house on her own were coming to an end. Surely, she would want to sell to someone that the house meant something to, someone who would give a fair price and could even help Estelle with the transition.

If Jenny was honest with herself, she would admit that she really had no intentions of staying and this would make it easier for her to leave again.

But in the meantime, she had made a valid point. As long as he was here with his daughters, he had to do his best to put his worries to the side and concentrate on giving them a joyous Christmas.

The problem of finding a new location for his business would not be going anywhere.

"You're right," he repeated to Jenny, watching her teasing expression be replaced by one that was attentive but cautious. Even before she reached up to unconsciously tug at her hair, one of her tells for uneasiness, he had known she would.

"You're right that the girls deserve Christmas, and I was hoping we could find one here in the midst of everything else going on. But, the state of the house is worse than I expected."

"Why do you think I came home?" Jenny said, with no accusation in her voice, just a quiet acknowledgment that things weren't the way they were supposed to be.

And probably hadn't been for a long time.

She is someone you once cared for very much. Can't you try to see things from her side?

He silently apologized to God for his critical spirit that insisted that Jenny wasn't being honest with herself when he could say the same about himself. Because this wasn't just about the girls—although they played a large role in it—it was also about him hoping to find the inner strength to make the right decisions about his next steps.

Because whether he bought Christmas House or not, change was coming, bearing down on him like a freight train, ready or not.

"Jenny," David said, hesitating as he hoped the urging he could feel in his heart expressed itself properly through his words, "I would love…" He stopped and started again. "I *need* this Christmas to be a good one. Can we please call a truce? I'd love it if you could help make Christmas here for my girls the way we remember it."

"There's so much to do," Jenny said, looking around. He noted the panic in her eyes. "And not a lot of time."

"We'll do it together," David said firmly, not letting himself dwell on how saying those words made him feel.

How many times had he said those words, or something similar, in the past and it had all amounted to nothing?

"I suppose if we got the girls to help," Jenny said hesitantly, "we could make it all part of the experience." Her eyes softened in thought. "Gran always used to save some things for me to do when I came over. I always got to put the star on the tree, and even if she'd already done some baking, she'd never decorate the cookies without me."

"Looks like that tradition could continue," David said, gesturing his head toward where his daughters and Estelle waited expectantly at the table.

"Go ahead and start," Jenny called over to them, then added to David in a lower tone, "I want to get this settled. We don't have a lot of time," she reiterated, getting the concentrated, almost fierce expression he recognized from when she was planning. He had seen that expression countless times from the little shows they'd put on for the neighbors when they were children to pushing to meet the deadline to get the yearbook to the printer in their senior year.

"We'll start with decorating the cookies," she continued musingly. "Then the girls can help me finish decorating the tree and the rest of the house. We can maybe see if the sleigh rides are all booked—oh, and we'll need to hit some of the shops for Christmas goodies."

David wondered what all the *we* business was about. It was more than a little disconcerting.

She stopped talking, shaking her head with a bemused expression. "Of course, I'm just assuming that the sleigh rides and the Christmas treats are still a thing here. I have no idea, except I know Graham's is decorated. I saw it when I was there."

"They are," David confirmed, "bigger and better than ever, as a matter of fact. A lot of the shops really go all out with Christmas decorations. It's become a little competitive," he said, laughing softly. "But it's fun for the rest of us."

"So maybe you and the girls have already done that?" Jenny asked, her wistful tone answering his previous unasked question.

She wants to find her place here again.

But he wouldn't let emotion control him. Sure, Jenny might be feeling nostalgic right now, but that would pass soon enough, and she'd get restless about leaving again.

"We haven't done them yet this year," he answered brusquely, shifting his eyes slightly down and to the right, so the light in her brilliant blue ones wouldn't make him forget that he'd made a promise to himself to shove her out of his heart and keep the door firmly locked.

"Oopsy-daisy!" Estelle caroled out cheerfully, and both David and Jenny swung their heads around just in time to see a bowl of sprinkles tip over and cascade colorfully all over the floor.

Rowena and Reba, immediately dropped to their knees and began the futile task of trying to gather them by hand while Jenny's grandmother giggled before her face suddenly drooped in tearful sadness.

"I'll get the broom," David murmured to Jenny. "Go see to your grandmother. Girls," he added, "we appreciate the effort but you can't pick them up by hand. You can go sit in the living room."

When he returned with the broom, Jenny sat holding the older woman's hand. Estelle appeared calm again, but Jenny's face was drawn and troubled.

He silently swept the sprinkles into the dustpan, as his mind raced. Trying to gain some clarity on the situation, he reached out in prayer.

Dear Lord, I don't want to misread Your messages, as I think I sometimes do, but I do feel like You're telling me to reach out in some way.

Just then, Jenny said to him, "I need help."

He nodded, and agreed with her. "You do." Her features softened when she saw that he wasn't being critical, just honest.

But he also prayed that the fact that he was more concerned than he wanted to be about her wasn't also showing on his face.

Estelle had calmed down again and said, "Well, are we going to finish decorating the cookies or what?"

"In a minute, Gran," Jenny told her. "David and I just have a little something to work out. I can take you to sit with the girls in the living room, if you like."

"I'll take myself," Estelle sniffed haughtily and stood up.

She took a couple of steps forward, then stopped and turned back, her eyes alert.

"Whatever it is," she said, "it will all work out." She gave one satisfied nod and left the room.

"Will she be okay?" David asked, then answered himself. "I'm sure the girls will let us know if she needs anything."

"That's what's so hard," Jenny said, pushing the heel of her hand against her forehead.

"What's so hard?" he asked, although he was pretty sure he already knew the answer. He did not like still being able to read her face like a map, knowing what each nuance of expression, every gesture meant.

"One minute she's like how she always was. Just Gran," Jenny answered. "And the next minute, something goes wrong."

"It's just some sprinkles on the floor," David pointed out, knowing what she meant, but trying to help her avoid sinking into panic. She had often commented on the calming force he had in her life.

But he was just trying to walk in the Lord's footsteps,

he told himself, to be a kind and giving person. It didn't mean anything more than that.

"But next time it could be something worse," Jenny said. "Look at what happened to me on the attic stairs, and you with the balcony door. This place is falling apart around us. But you and your girls deserve Christmas too. I just don't know what to do."

"You let me help you fix up the place," David said firmly, speaking quickly while Jenny was somewhat receptive.

"But I don't want to owe you," Jenny said. "I don't want you to think it means that I'm selling you this house."

"It's not yours to sell," David couldn't help reminding her, the way Gran had reminded them both.

Her eyes shot bright blue sparks, but before she could say anything he offered an apologetic smile.

"Let's just make Christmas for my girls and your Gran…please?"

Jenny eyed him warily but after a moment said, "We never did talk about what my part is supposed to be in all this. I mean, if you're helping around the house."

David hardly knew he was going to say it until it came out of his mouth.

"I thought maybe you could spend time with Reba, share what you've been through, let her know it's going to be all right. With Rowe too," he added. "You were always good with kids that felt…left out."

As soon as he said the words, he regretted them. He didn't want his daughters forming any kind of attachment to her nor her to them. Not to mention he didn't have any idea how life had gone for Jenny since her cancer diagnosis, because she had never spoken to him about it.

But when he saw her wariness replaced by surprise and something else, something that mixed hope and regret in a bittersweet combination, he knew he couldn't take the words back.

He would just have to hope and pray they all got through this unscathed.

Chapter Six

The next morning, a Saturday, Jenny pulled on one of her favorite Christmas sweaters, the one with the dancing elves and reindeer, and yanked it over her head, following up with a spritz of water and a hastily wielded hairbrush. Then she went into the bathroom and brushed her teeth. Gran had been invited to have lunch with the pastor and his wife , and while Jenny was happy for her to have some diversion, it made going on an outing with David Hart and his daughters that much more conspicuous. She was careful to avoid looking at her reflection because if she didn't see her own eyes, she wouldn't see the trepidation in them.

If she could just pretend that she wasn't feeling a certain way, then she didn't have to confront it.

She'd be perfectly fine with the fact that she and David Hart and his daughters were about to head to town for their first round of Christmas events and that everyone would see them together and make all kinds of assumptions. But unless Living Skies had changed a whole lot since she'd left, which she highly doubted, everyone would have all kinds of questions for her, and it made her shudder to even imagine answering them.

Well, you see, I'm home because my Gran needs me, but I had no idea how bad things were. Also, did I mention that I have nowhere else to go because I was fired from my last job and I drained my savings account to travel?

She knew that Gran would tell her to take her worries to the Lord, but she wondered if Gran herself was remembering to do that.

Church with Gran had always been a more open and joyful experience than church with her parents. There was no denying that they were passionate believers—they structured their whole lives around their faith, after all—but Jenny could never just talk to God like He was her friend when she was with them, the way she did with Gran.

"Dad, can we go soon?" Rowe's plaintive voice floated up the stairs to remind Jenny that she had better get going.

She dared one quick glance at her eyes, which betrayed her efforts to act like this was no big deal, and scurried down the stairs. The banister wobbled under her hand as she descended, and she made a mental note.

At this rate, David was going to be fixing things until Easter.

The three faces waiting for her at the bottom of the stairs made Jenny want to turn around and go back to bed.

David looked good, too good, in a toasted-brown pullover sweater that picked up the lighter hues in his deep brown eyes.

He looked so handsome, so grown-up, which she knew was a silly thought to have, because naturally they had both grown up. Since high school, they'd both lived their lives and had countless experiences that the other hadn't been part of, even though they had once had an unspoken promise to share everything.

At the moment, however, she was doing her best impersonation of an eight-year-old in her goofy sweater. Even Rowena and Reba were dressed in more grown-up clothing than she was, wearing respectively hunter green and mint green long-sleeved jerseys under gray down-filled vests. Brightly colored winter hats, Rowe's with geometric shapes and Reba's with snowflakes, adorned their heads.

Jenny noticed David struggling not to laugh when he saw her sweater. He managed to restrain himself but was unable to resist commenting, "I see some things never change."

"Hey, you rocked a mean ugly sweater yourself back in the day," she reminded him, pushing back against the flush of unexpected bashfulness.

"What do you mean *back in the day*?" Rowe asked. Her voice made an attempt at casualness, but her eyes were sharp arrows darting between them, trying to find their mark.

"Jenny and I have known each other since we were kids," David explained. He conveyed the easy assurance of a parent who'd had years of practice answering his children's questions.

"Jenny's Gran said that you were probably going to get married because you used to be in love and probably still were." Reba's eyes looked between them anxiously, but it was hard to tell whether she hoped for confirmation or denial.

David's in-control-dad vibe appeared to waver for a moment before he snapped to again.

"Estelle is getting older," he explained. "And sometimes older people get a little confused about things. It's not her fault."

Sure, throw Gran under the bus, Jenny thought. Yet, what else was there for him to say?

"Dad's not going to get married again, silly," Rowe said firmly.

"But did you and Jenny used to date each other?" Reba asked.

Jenny caught David's eye and silently asked him to make the call. He was their father, after all, and it was up to him what his daughters knew and didn't know.

"We did date each other," David confirmed. "But that was a long time ago, and no, I don't plan on getting married again, to Jenny or anyone else. I'm happy just being with my girls."

He reached out his arms and pulled them both into a side hug. Reba giggled and collapsed into him, but Rowena squirmed away.

"Can we get going or what?" she whined.

"I think that's a great idea," David said, clearly relieved that the subject had been dropped. But Rowe's attitude niggled at Jenny. It was sad enough if an adult decided that he wasn't willing to take another chance on love anymore, but to hear an eight-year-old girl make that assumption troubled her.

But it wasn't her place to say anything. Even if she could, how could she raise the question of doubts about love to the girl's father when she was the one who had left him?

But he had moved on from her, she reminded herself. He had fallen in love again, married and had two beautiful daughters. She'd had her reasons for leaving and was still sure that if she had a do-over, she would make the same choice.

So why did small currents of hurt still move through her?

"Okay, first stop on our tour of Christmas decor and goodies is Graham's Grocers! Who's with me?" said Jenny.

Gran had been invited to the pastor's house for lunch so would not be joining them.

"It's not my favorite," Rowe muttered.

Lord, please help me to be patient and understanding. I know that her attitude is coming from a place of pain, and we've all got a lot to deal with right now. I can't do this without Your grace.

She did believe that Rowe needed her at least as much as her sister did.

Or needs someone, she quickly corrected herself.

"Are you kidding?" she asked with exaggerated shock. "Graham's looks fantastic this year. Wait until you see it. And no one makes a cup of hot cocoa like Wilson does."

She was playing up her enthusiasm for a trip to Graham's because Fern already knew that David and the twins were staying at Christmas House, so she was hopeful that would help postpone any awkward explanations. On the other hand, Graham's was bound to be teeming with customers, which was maybe not such a bad thing, because then it could be like ripping off a bandage dealing with everybody's questions at once. Or maybe she was being ridiculously self-absorbed to think that anyone was all that interested in her return home or in her relationship with David Hart.

David cleared his throat softly. "Should we go?"

"Yes, yes, we should get going," Jenny agreed hastily. She gave up on her sales pitch, deciding that Graham's was perfectly capable of doing its own dazzling. Besides, what was she doing, newly back in town, trying to sell them on what they should and shouldn't be doing?

The deal was, she reminded herself, that David would help get the house in order, and she would be there if Reba needed someone to talk to who had been through the disease and was also a survivor. If she could, she also wanted to help Rowena shrug off some of that cynicism that made her too old for her age.

She could only hope and pray that the arrangement would keep their tentative civility in place.

David and the girls walked a couple of steps ahead of her, and she watched as Rowe pulled her hand away from her father's grip and picked up a snowball, which she turned and threw, with surprisingly lethal aim, in Jenny's direction.

Jenny's reflexes were excellent, however, and she jerked to the right just in time to have the snowball whiz past her ear rather than get a cold, wet slap in the face.

Once again, she was sure that she had at least as much in common with Rowe as she did with Reba.

Realizing what was happening, David spun around. "Rowe," he exclaimed. "What are you doing? You could have hurt Jenny. Are you okay?" he asked her.

She laughed as she bent down and began to gather snow. When she stood up she saw Rowe watching her, pulsing with pent-up energy, holding her own snowball, and noticed that David and Reba were laughing and busily packing their own ammunition.

After David called out the quick rule that aiming at

someone's face was not allowed, the snowballs flew with abandon, and soon Rowena joined in with her own unrestrained giggle, a blissful sound, alongside her sister's.

Jenny gave a sigh of relief and thanked God that she had been able to turn the moment into something fun and silly for them all to share. Because it hadn't escaped her attention that Rowe's first throw wasn't completely without malice. Despite her *whatever* attitude, trying to come across like she didn't care, Jenny was sure that she struggled hugely with her mother's absence and did not want anyone to take her place.

Jenny's heart ached for her. She knew how devastating it was to resent a parent's absence while, at the same time, desperately longing for them to be present.

She had absolutely no intentions of being part of David's life. But when she saw him with his eyes crinkled in laughter, it was like seeing him as a boy again, her best friend, her first love.

Then, his laughter faltered and abruptly halted. "Reba, are you okay? Reba?"

Jenny hurried over. Reba had gone pale and was shakily trying to capture air into her lungs.

"She's just overexerted herself a bit," Jenny said, rapidly surveying the girl for signs she had been taught to watch for in herself. No doubt David must have been taught the same thing. Some of it he would have learned from her while she was going through her own battle. But, she could only imagine, that wasn't quite the same as watching your own child go through it.

Her own parents had been stoic, giving praise and thanks to the Lord for the healing they anticipated He would provide. Jenny was grateful for their faith, but part of her had longed for them to show that they would be shattered by losing her. Even just a little bit.

So, she took a moment to savor David's obvious concern, even as her shoulders tightened in sorrow and her throat burned with the loss of something she knew she would never get back.

"This is normal," Jenny reassured him. She caught herself from reminding him *Don't you remember how exhausted I was?* "Well, not normal," she hastily added. "Nothing about cancer is normal."

At one time in their lives, she and David could have and probably would have launched into a hearty debate about God and His purposes and why bad things happened to good people. But, ultimately, they would both conclude that, although God could be a mystery, they believed beyond anything that His son Jesus embodied and demonstrated His undying love for them all and they couldn't imagine their lives without Him.

These days she struggled a bit with that undying-love concept, and it was easy to imagine that David might too, going through Reba's illness and the subsequent departure of his wife. Maybe one day they would talk about it.

Despite her faith wavering like the streams of pale sunlight that appeared and disappeared on a cloudy day, Jenny paused to offer up prayer on behalf of David and his daughters.

"Her color is coming back," Jenny said, hoping that she sounded reassuring.

Reba's breathing regulated, and a grin spread across her face.

"That was completely *awesome*!" she exclaimed.

The others burst into relieved laughter.

"You're such a dork," Rowe said, with affection. She looped her arm through her twin's, and they all continued their walk toward the grocery store.

Jenny sidled up to David.

"I didn't mean to stick my nose in," she said after they'd gone a few steps in silence.

"I know," David said. "But I really appreciated that you knew what she needed."

They were simple words, but they warmed her. Maybe things would be okay between them, after all.

If he hadn't known that Jenny hadn't been home for years, David wouldn't have guessed it by watching her interact with the other citizens of Living Skies who had streamed into Graham's to gape at the decorations, sample the cookies from the myriad platters, and warm up with their choice of coffee, cinnamon tea or hot chocolate.

Watching her work the crowd, he remembered how she had always been able to win people over. They never saw her nervousness the way he did or knew the amount of pep-talking she had to give herself.

But I don't really know her anymore.

Still, he knew it couldn't be easy, coming back, dealing with the curiosity and speculation of the town.

David himself had questions.

He knew why she was back—at least, what she'd said—which was to be with Estelle. But, really, there had been plenty of opportunities to do that over the years, and she had never done so. He couldn't help wondering exactly what—*or who*—had kept her away.

Jenny had always been a talented writer, and David recalled that on one of the last times they had discussed their dreams and goals, she had talked about wanting to write stories that made a difference in people's lives. In high school, being so involved in sports had taken up a lot of her time, but her stories were often featured in the school paper, and she'd also written for the yearbook.

For a time, after she was gone, he found himself searching newspapers and magazines for her name, but it was like constantly poking at a wound, and he honestly didn't know if he was relieved or disappointed when she didn't see her byline, so eventually he stopped doing it.

Despite Rowena's declarations of being less than impressed with the store, once they were inside she bounced on her heels and yanked at Reba's hand. "Let's go get some treats."

"Be careful," David said. He meant with Reba, but then seeing the exasperated—and slightly forlorn look— on Rowe's face, he amended. "I just mean there are a lot of people here. Be careful that you don't bump into any of them with hot drinks. Come right back here when you're done at the refreshment table."

"Or we could just go with them," Jenny suggested.

"I'm surprised you would want to," David said, bluntly. "Aren't you trying to avoid the town gossip?"

Her smile collapsed, but she quickly recovered and said, "Well, I plan to head over there too, and unless you've lost your sweet tooth, which I doubt, I think you'll probably want to go with me."

"I haven't lost it," David said, allowing a slight smile. "In fact, I think it may have gotten worse over the years."

"Ahh, so you're still paying for Dr. Bennett's winter vacations," Jenny quipped, naming the town's dentist, who had been in Living Skies so long that he had ended up treating several generations of townspeople.

Just then, her eyes went anxious. "|He didn't retire, did he?"

"No," David said. "Feel free to get as many cavities as you want." He attempted to keep the lightheartedness of the conversation going, but it was just a reminder that she hadn't been in Living Skies for years.

"Well, that's a relief," Jenny said.

There was a beat of silence, then gesturing toward the back of the store, David said, "Shall we?"

Wilson Graham waited there behind a table of hot drinks and goodies. He leaned on a cane, which briefly made him look older than his sixty-nine years, but when a grin lit up his face, he was the Wilson they had always known.

David spotted Rowe and Reba a couple of people ahead of them. They were clutching hands and chatting excitedly, pointing at the tables, no doubt trying to decide which of the bounty of treats to try first.

His heart sang to see that they still had a bond between them even if it was as fragile as some of the glass ornaments that hung on the tree

"Well, well," Wilson called out. "Jenny Powell and David Hart. Now, there's a familiar sight if I ever saw one."

David wondered how he had managed to forget just how Wilson's voice carried.

A brief glance at Jenny told him that she was thinking exactly the same thing, which suddenly made it seem kind of hilarious.

"Hey, Wilson!" she called out with aplomb that David admired, even as it put them in the spotlight of several curious stares. Even his daughters swiveled to take a look.

"Fern told me you were back in town, |Jenny," he called back. "It's good to see it with my own eyes."

"It's good to be back," Jenny said, not adding, as David expected her to, that it was only temporary.

"Jenny?" They turned and saw a tall, red-haired woman with a freckled face, towing a redheaded boy who was a miniature version of herself. The little boy had a candy cane in each fist and a telltale gloss of stickiness around his mouth.

"I can't believe you're here," the woman said excitedly. "It's Nancy Chamberlain. I used to be Nancy Boyd We were in some classes together, and I helped on the school paper."

"Of course I remember you, Nancy," Jenny said, drawing her into a warm hug.

"Hi, David," Nancy said as she and Jenny separated from their hug. "It's good to see you too. Are you two...?" She pointed a finger back and forth between them in speculation.

"No," they both said at the same time.

"It's nothing like that that," Jenny added for good measure.

"Can't blame a gal for wondering," Nancy said, unfazed. "Hey!" She snapped her fingers. "Some of the other girls from high school are here, and I know they'd love to see you."

Nancy looked around, her pale blue eyes behind tortoiseshell glasses searching the crowd. Meanwhile, her son solemnly studied his candy canes.

"Oh, there's Becca," Nancy said. "Becca, over here!" she waved frantically.

David noticed that Jenny's jaw was clenching, and her eyes had something of the look of the proverbial deer in the headlights.

"I really hate to break up a reunion, ladies," he said, "but Jenny promised to help my girls make decorations at the arts-and-crafts table, didn't you, Jen?"

Jenny's face broke out into a beaming smile of gratitude. David wasn't even sure why he had rescued her, but he allowed the feeling of satisfaction to linger.

Nancy was too much of a gossip for his liking.

"Oh, are your twins here?|" Nancy gushed. "They are just the sweetest. How is poor little Reba doing these days?"

This time it was Jenny's turn to rescue him.

"Reba is a survivor," Jenny said in a firm, clear voice. "She's about the strongest kid you could meet. More of us would do well to handle our problems with that kind of strength and dignity."

Nancy laughed uneasily. Then her little boy accidentally dropped one of his candy canes on the floor and starting wailing.

"I think that's our cue," David murmured in Jenny's ear. In a louder voice he said, "There are the girls now." He spotted Rowe and Reba heading their way, each with a Christmasy mug in one hand and a colorfully decorated cookie in the other.

"Nancy, it was so great to see you," Jenny added. "Please do say hi to everyone for me."

Nancy nodded as she walked away with her son.

When they were out of earshot, Jenny said to him, "Thank you for doing that."

"You're welcome. And thank you for what you said about Reba."

"I only spoke the truth," Jenny said, softly.

The twins joined them.

"What are you talking about?" asked the ever-watchful Rowe.

"Old friends," David answered promptly. His eyes met Jenny's for a moment before he looked away again.

"So what treats did you get?" he asked his daughters.

"Gingerbread," said Reba.

"Sugar cookie," answered Rowe.

"Looks good," David said. "And how's the hot chocolate? Does Wilson still live up to his reputation? And, most importantly, marshmallows or whipped cream?"

"Both!" his daughters said, giggling.

Behind his banter, though, David's emotions whirled with the connection that was clearly still present between him and Jenny. They should not still be able to read each other so well, not after fifteen years apart.

"You don't really have to help the girls with crafts, you know," he said, trying to re-erect the barrier he had worked so carefully to build.

But Reba's face lit up. "Crafts? Can we?"

"What about you?" he asked Rowe. "Feel like making an ornament or two?"

"I guess I could," Rowe said, her shining eyes belying her attempt at a careless tone.

David didn't want to disappoint his daughters but promised himself that he would continue to keep his distance from Jenny as best he could and make sure Rowe and Reba knew she wasn't going to be around for long.

Chapter Seven

Seeing the craft table that was set up against one of the side walls—a canned-goods display had been moved to accommodate it—gave Jenny another jolt of home-coming, and again the ache of regret surged through her bones.

The long, low table had folding chairs lined up on either side, where people of all ages happily worked and exclaimed over each other's creations.

A red paper tablecloth covered the table, which offered an almost mind-boggling array of ribbons, balls, glitter and stars in a multitude of colors, along with several bottles of glue, pairs of scissors, rolls of tape, even balls of string. To complete the Christmas crafters' dreams were bowls of cranberries and popcorn for stringing.

Jenny and the girls found chairs toward the far end of the table. David hovered as if uncertain what to do, and Jenny said, "Are you going to join us?"

She could see the struggle on his face. "It's totally up to you," she added.

David lowered himself to a chair too quickly, as if

doing so before he had a chance to change his mind. The chair wobbled and tipped as he caught the edge of it and fell backward, leaving him in an awkward squatting position.

Jenny leaped up from her own chair and set the errant chair upright again.

"Daaad!" Rowena wailed, as her father lowered himself into the chair. "You're so embarrassing."

"It could happen to anyone," Jenny said. "These chairs are really shaky."

She had meant well, but the look he shot her was a clear message that he didn't need her support, especially not when it involved his daughters.

Rowe and Reba were selecting supplies for their ornaments as Jenny pulled out two large silver baubles, some royal blue glitter and streams of blue and silver ribbon.

"I thought you'd go for the popcorn," David remarked quietly.

Jenny turned to look at him. His brown eyes weren't exactly apologetic, but they were softer, and she remembered as kids, sitting at the dining-room table at Gran's, eating about as much popcorn as they were stringing, and laughing with the pure joy of two young people with nothing but time and adventures ahead of them.

"Uh...thanks for the chair thing," David mumbled. "As you can see, the passage of time hasn't made me any more graceful. No wonder I went out for debate while you were rocking all those sports."

Jenny smiled. "As I said, it could have happened to anyone."

The twins were already fully engaged in their projects. With her brow furrowed in concentration, Rowe carefully glued silver stars onto a large red bauble, while Reba tied a green ribbon around a small gold box to represent a present under the Christmas tree.

On a sudden whim, Jenny picked up a ball of string, unraveled it and indicated that David should take the other end.

He did so, his eyebrows quirked in a question.

"Shall we?" She pointed at the bowl of popcorn.

No big deal, she told herself, but she had to admit she was on pins and needles waiting for his answer.

He studied her for a long moment, then glanced at his girls who were still engrossed in their projects.

"Give me that bowl," he said.

Jenny had to tame the wide smile that wanted to run wild across her face. She pushed the bowl toward him.

He promptly grabbed a handful of popcorn and munched on it before getting down to business.

"Some things never change," Jenny said, rolling her eyes.

They worked in compatible silence, and Jenny was grateful, but after a little while, her worries about Gran, the house and what she would do if she stayed in Living Skies came to mind. Where would she work? How would she find the money that would surely be needed to keep the house up and running, even if David did help with some of the repairs?

If Gran eventually did end up in a care facility, they were usually so expensive. How would she ever afford it?

She knew she had never been good about saving money, but after she'd gone into remission, she'd only wanted to live in the moment, take chances and trust that God would provide and help get her to the next place she wanted to be in her life.

It wasn't as easy anymore to have that kind of trust.

"You're slacking off,|" David said, pointing at her hands that had gone still. "What's the matter?"

There was a time she would have welcomed the opportunity to pour her heart out to him, including the fact that she had no job to return to, no home other than the one she prayed wouldn't be taken from her.

"I was just thinking that I hope Gran's having fun at Pastor |Liam's for lunch and that everything is okay with her."

"I'm sure she's having a great time," David said reassuringly. "She still loves church. When she's there, it's like she's young again."

The popcorn and cranberry string was finished and lay between them. The twins had finished their ornaments too but appeared content to start on another craft.

"So you still go to church regularly?" Jenny asked tentatively.

David shrugged. "Sure," he said. "I mean, it's kind of a habit after all these years, and the girls enjoy Sunday school."

A wave of sadness engulfed Jenny at hearing the boy she'd so passionately debated faith with referring to church as a *habit*, because no matter where their arguments took them, at the core of it all, they both knew the other had a living faith.

Still, she wasn't one to talk: her church attendance had been spotty at best during her travels over the years, and, even when she did go, there were times she found herself questioning what it really meant to her.

"What about you?" David asked. "Or were you too busy on your glamorous world travels?"

His tone was bright, but the light didn't reach his eyes.

There was so much she could have told him, but all she said was, "I managed to find some churches." Then she added, "And it wasn't always all that glamorous."

David picked up the almost-empty popcorn bowl in an absent-minded way and ate the few remaining pieces.

Jenny remembered that when his forehead furrowed and his mouth worked in a certain way, it meant that David was having an inner debate about something.

"What exactly *were* you doing all these years?" he asked finally, still gazing into the now-empty bowl and not at her.

There was a world of questions within that one, so much that needed to be said and so much lost time between them.

"Traveling, " she said vaguely. "Working here and there."

"What kind of work?"

Jenny shifted in her chair and snatched up another ball of string, which she nervously started to unravel, even though there was no popcorn left.

"Oh, this and that," she said. "Mostly odd jobs, whatever I could find for work. I was even a hotel maid for a little while, though that didn't last long."

"So you never did anything with your writing?" The area between David's deep brown eyes furrowed, and Jenny knew he must be wondering what could possibly have kept her away for so long if it wasn't pursuing the dream to write—the dream she had so often shared with him.

She wished she knew the answer to that herself. She'd

say just about anything to chase that look away from his eyes.

"Dad, can we go to some of the other stores soon?"

Never would Jenny have thought she'd be so glad to hear Rowena's demanding voice.

"Sure," David said, suddenly standing up from his chair. "Where would you like to go next?"

When he turned to Jenny and said, "Don't feel obligated to join us," the message in his stony face was clear.

The hurt she swallowed tasted bitter, even though she couldn't blame him. She stood up and tilted her chin to meet his eyes.

"You all go ahead and have fun. Maybe I'll hang out here a little bit longer and catch up with Nancy and her crew."

David's eyes widened for a brief second before he recovered and said, "Say hi to them for me."

Only Reba had asked if Jenny was sure she didn't want to come with them, and she was such a sweet girl that Jenny was sure she would have extended the invitation to anyone.

After they left the grocery store, she checked her watch. There was still plenty of time before she had to be home for Gran getting dropped off. Time stretched out before her like a long, empty road, reminding her that she no longer fit in this town.

But she had to make her place here again. She didn't have any other options.

Then Jenny spotted Grace Severight, carrying a big garbage bag and loading discarded paper plates and utensils and remaining scraps from the craft table into it. Their store's Christmas open house was a time when the Grahams welcomed anyone who wanted to pitch in on clean-up.

Jenny inwardly breathed a brief prayer of thanks at the sight of a familiar and trusted face.

Although Jenny had been well-known through her sports and activities in high school, and generally well-liked, she was more reserved than people realized, choosing carefully who she really opened up to.

There was no question that David Hart was at the top of that list, and the uneasiness between them now pained her.

It was just like practical Grace, Jenny thought with a smile, to get ahead of the clean-up so that it wasn't all left until the end. She recalled numerous high-school and church youth-group gatherings where Grace had kept busy in the kitchen, washing glasses and plates almost as soon as they had been used.

Jenny approached her friend. "Could you use a hand?"

"Jenny! Hi!" Grace put down the bag and hugged her.

Jenny returned the hug, clinging for an extra second. It felt wonderful to see a friendly face, someone who was actually happy to see her.

When they separated, Grace studied her with a puzzled smile.

She was of medium height and pretty in a simple, unadorned way, with light green eyes and slightly tousled wavy brown hair. Grace Severight might look like someone who would fit in playing volleyball on the beach.

"What's up?" she asked. "It's like you just jumped off the *Titanic* and I'm the last lifeboat in sight."

Jenny sighed and shook her head.

"It's nothing," she said. "How have *you* been? And, seriously, where can I get one of those garbage bags?"

"If you're serious, walk this way." Grace led her to a back storage room that was filled with cleaning supplies.

As they circulated cleaning together, Grace caught her up with news of her putting in an application to be a foster parent and the start of a new women's Bible study at the church.

"I did see Nancy," Jenny said, which caused Grace to crinkle her nose.

Jenny laughed. "You got that right."

"I saw you at the craft table with David Hart and his daughters," Grace said.

Jenny's hand froze in midair, transferring a bedraggled piece of garland into the bag she carried.

A thousand responses seemed to rush into Jenny's mind at the same time, none of them adequate, because none of them helped her decide if she wanted to hide or express her loss and confusion.

"Did you know they're staying at my Gran's house?" she finally said. "A pipe burst at their house, and that's where they ended up."

"Really?" Grace paused her own cleaning. "Why not a hotel, or at his parents' place?"

Jenny shrugged. "He says Gran invited him—and, trust me, that's a whole other story—and I guess he thought it would be fun for the girls to experience Christmas House—"

"Oh, is Estelle doing Christmas House this year?" Grace interjected. "I passed by there the other day on my run, and it didn't really look like too many decorations had been put up."

Unbidden tears sprung into Jenny's eyes.

"Hey," Grace said. "Let's go sit down for a minute. It's probably too early to be cleaning up anyway. There are still a lot of people here."

Jenny felt her cheeks turn hot and her eyes fill with tears. She didn't cry in public—*ever*.

Except now, apparently.

"Come on," Grace took her elbow and steered her toward some chairs that were stacked against the back wall, grabbed two of them and gestured for Jenny to sit down.

"Okay, so what is it?" Grace asked. "And don't bother saying *it's nothing* because I won't believe you."

"It's—" Jenny drew in a shuddering breath and exhaled "—it's everything."

She found herself pouring out her ever-increasing concerns about Gran, the fact that she didn't have a job, and finally, with the reluctance of something being lifted out of hardening cement, she dragged it out of herself how difficult the situation was with David.

Grace listened, attentive and silent, not saying anything until Jenny had finished.

"What I often tell my physical-therapy patients," she said then, "is *one step at a time*, and I don't mean that just literally. I mean that there's no denying that their lives have changed and they have a lot to deal with, a lot to figure out, but they'll get there. They might not believe it at the time, but they will get there. And eventually, one step at a time, they start to believe that they will get there. So what's your first step, Jenny?"

Jenny shrugged and sniffled a little, then hiccupped, which made her giggle a little.

"I wish I knew, Grace," she said. "But I'm sure I'll

figure it out. Thanks for listening. I'm done with this self-pity party."

"Anytime," Grace said and patted her hand. "People sometimes put up Help Wanted and employment ads on a bulletin board in the clinic. If I see anything I think you might be interested in, I'll give you a call."

"Thank you, Grace," Jenny said. "I really appreciate it."

"And about David," Grace added. "He certainly doesn't hate you."

"Why do you say that?"

"Anyone who looks at you the way he still does… Well, let's just say it's a long way from hate."

Grace had to be wrong, Jenny thought as they resumed cleaning. Was it her imagination, or was she trying to make Jenny feel better?

Besides, why should she care how David looked at her? Those days were long gone.

Weren't they?

Except, every time she thought about Grace's words, part of her wanted to take the broom she now held and dance it across the room.

Then she remembered the look on David's face when he found out that she hadn't pursued any kind of writing career. She remembered Gran's issues and that she was unemployed with no immediate prospects in sight.

The broom did its job as it was supposed to, a silent and bleak partner.

It seemed that with every store they went into, the bustling Christmas crowds increased, the music was louder, the decorations more extravagant, the cookies sweeter and the dollops of whipped cream on the hot chocolate more generous.

Although David found himself unable to enjoy any of it, for the sake of the girls—it *was* such a treat to see them actually enjoying the same thing at the same time—he made appropriate expressions of enthusiasm, while his mind was a million miles away.

For years, really, he realized, right up until their very recent conversation, he had coped with Jenny's absence by imagining that she was following her dreams. He was still hurt and angry over the way she had left, and he still wished that she had chosen him, but somehow, telling himself that she had gone off to achieve a goal that, for whatever reason, she'd decided she couldn't pursue in Living Skies, had made her leaving him, her Gran, and her other friends and family just a little bit more bearable.

And now, to find out that she'd stayed away for fifteen years working a string of jobs that did nothing to move her closer to her writing goals...

He had a sudden suspicion then that she had come home because of financial problems.

"Dad?" Reba said, "I'm going over there."

They were currently in The Play's The Thing toy store and she pointed to a wall of porcelain dolls dressed in their best Christmas finery.

"Dolls," Rowena sniffed, but she followed her sister.

"Okay," David said. "Don't go anywhere else without letting me know."

He forced his thoughts away from Jenny Powell. It didn't matter whether she was cleaning hotel rooms or winning a Pulitzer Prize. She had made the choice that she didn't want him to be part of her life.

Besides, he certainly had enough in his own life to deal with. Yes, there had been many happy moments without her, but his life was now fraying at the edges with a concerning number of problems. He was currently without the comfort of a home—not that the one he lived in was bringing much comfort these days. He had some time off for the holiday season, but with the nature of his work, that didn't mean that he wasn't on call and could be needed at any time.

He loved his work, but lately he didn't find it as fulfilling, and he wondered if that was why finding a new location seemed difficult.

He wished he could figure out what was missing because, for as long as he could remember, he'd wanted to help and protect people, and that hadn't changed.

A sharp prickle like something blowing a blast of icy air made David reach his hand back quickly to massage his neck.

Who had been there to protect Jenny?

It was unnerving to realize that the thought of anyone, or any situation, harming Jenny Powell in any way still made his throat tighten and his fists clench.

Once again, he reminded himself that she wasn't part of his life and that he had his own problems to deal with.

Speaking of which…was that Bruce Willoughby across the room, holding a Santa mug and clearly telling some anecdote to an appreciative audience?

Bruce had always had a knack for storytelling, which David appreciated as well…unless, of course, the busy contractor was supposed to be at his house making it habitable again.

David mentally calculated the impact of a confrontation. His eyes went to his daughters.

Reba beamed at a porcelain doll wearing a green-and-red plaid dress with matching ribbons in its fake gold ringlets. Rowe maintained an air of nonchalance but then, ever so slowly, reached out to gently touch the silver lace on the skirt of another doll.

That made David's decision for him. He would deal with Bruce another time.

But it also reminded him that the days were speeding by and that he'd better get going on a backup plan for office space and maybe for other temporary living quarters as well.

Because he wasn't at all sure anymore that Jenny and he were going to manage the Christmas season together, despite the tentative truce they'd made.

Later, after they had made a couple more quick stops, Reba said with forced brightness, "I'd be okay to go back to the house now. I mean, if you guys want to."

"That means she's ready for her afternoon nap," Rowe said.

David observed Reba's pallor and the shadows under her eyes.

"We could all use a nap after all those cookies," he said, keeping his tone light. "I don't know about you, but right now I don't even want to see another Christmas cookie."

"I guess I'd be okay going home," Rowena said softly.

It was all too easy, and David wished that his girls could be swept up into the giddy excitement they had experienced a few years ago. Like the times when they would have eaten cookies until they were just about to burst and then refused to touch their suppers, or when they begged for certain gifts, exclaiming that they couldn't live without one toy and then another.

They were almost out the door when Bruce flagged David down.

"Just taking a little break," Bruce said in his boisterously cheerful way. "Hi, girls!"

They nodded and ducked their heads, even Rowena bashful in the presence of Bruce's significant height and girth and larger-than-life personality.

"I wasn't going to ask," David said with a tight smile.

"I had to order some parts," Bruce explained. "Everything's a backlog these days. You know how it is."

"Please just move things along as quickly as you can," David said. "The girls and I are anxious to get back home."

"Yup, you got it." Bruce then waggled his eyebrows, making them dance like dark and furry caterpillars on his forehead. "I hear that Jenny Powell is back."

"She is," David replied, not even bothering to force a smile this time. He had to send the message to Bruce and to anyone who asked him that he wasn't the least interested.

"Anyway, we have to get going,"

Before they were out the door, David could hear Bruce's raucous laugh ringing out as he entertained yet another group of eager listeners.

Was what he had said to Bruce even true? David wondered as they walked back toward Estelle's house.

Was it true that they were anxious to move back home? Of course, he wanted—needed—to get things fixed, no one could live in a house without properly working plumbing. But that didn't mean that it was still the home for him and his girls.

But if their house didn't feel like home anymore, where was home?

When they arrived back at Estelle's, the scent of peppermint greeted them, and despite his insistence that he couldn't eat another bite or take another sip, David found the aroma very appealing.

They found Jenny and Estelle in the kitchen. Jenny was serving her grandma a cup of peppermint tea.

David poked his head into the kitchen. "We're back," he said, directing his comment to Estelle who smiled at him. "I'm just going to get the girls settled in their room, then I'd like to hear all about your lunch with Pastor Liam and Carol."

"I don't need to be settled," Rowe grumbled, while Reba fought a yawn so hard that her face became a tight mask.

"Well, Reba needs to rest," David said. "You can grab a book and sit quietly down here, if you want."

"What are you drinking?" Rowena asked Jenny. "It smells like candy canes."

"It's peppermint tea."

Rowe scrunched up her nose. "I don't like tea."

Dear Lord, please give me patience, David prayed silently. "What's it going to be, Rowe? Reba needs to lie down. Would you like to rest too, or would you like to bring a book down here?"

Exhaling a long, huffy sigh, Rowe said, "I guess I'll hang out in our room."

As David followed them upstairs, he heard Reba's small, weary voice say "I'm sorry" to her sister, and his heart ached but he didn't interject because that would be sure to further tangle the fragile thread that still bound his twin daughters despite everything.

After the twins were in their room, he was tempted to go into his own, shut the door and avoid all the things he had to face—the decisions he had to make—for as long as he could.

But he had told Estelle he would be back and, besides, he was a grown-up, and facing tough things was what grown-ups did.

When David went back into the kitchen, Jenny was on her tiptoes reaching for something in one of the cupboards. The long, clean lines of her form reminded David of watching her play sports in high school, and he forced himself to look away, as unwanted emotions washed over him.

He focused on Estelle instead. "You were going to tell me about your lunch with the pastor and his wife," he prompted her, as he slid into a chair across from hers at the table.

Jenny asked, "Do you want tea? Or coffee?"

"No, thanks. I'm filled to the brim with cider and hot chocolate." David couldn't resist adding, "I thought you would be too."

Jenny joined them and carefully set the teacups down on the table.

"Careful," she said to Estelle, "it's hot." To David she said, "I helped Grace with clean-up. It helped me get at least a thirst back again."

"Grace and her cleaning," he smiled and shook his head.

They glanced at each other. There would always be memories between them, whether they wanted there to be or not.

Despite her own warning, Jenny took a too-hasty sip of her tea and grimaced.

David immediately leaped up to dash to the sink and run cold water into a glass for her.

She gulped it, her eyes watering over the rim, then finally managed to gasp, "Thank you."

"Not a problem," David tossed the words off lightly, while inwardly troubled at how naturally he'd come to her rescue.

She doesn't need rescuing, and I would have done the same for anyone.

Estelle watched all of this with an interested expression. Her own tea sat untouched.

"May I have a glass of milk please?" she asked, in an oddly formal way, as if she wasn't in her own home.

"I'll get it," Jenny said hastily.

Finally they were all settled with their beverages, and David reminded Estelle that she was going to tell them about her visit.

"Oh, it was lovely," Estelle said, sounding very pleased. "We had egg salad sandwiches and a fruit punch. Have you noticed that hardly anyone makes a nice egg salad anymore? It's a shame. It's such a tasty sandwich if it's done properly. Now, the secret to not getting that gray discoloration in the yolk is this—"

"Gran, was anyone else there at lunch?" Jenny prodded gently before her grandmother could go on about hard-boiled eggs. "What did Carol serve for dessert?"

"Besides me, the Russells were there." Estelle sounded brisk again, as she named a middle-aged couple from the congregation. Bill Russell was a manager at the local bank, and his wife, Vivian, worked as the receptionist at the town newspaper and was renowned for her soprano singing voice, which was an asset to the church choir.

"We had fresh fruit salad for dessert and some brownies, which I don't think were homemade but were still quite good. I told them," she added pointedly to Jenny, "that you'll be joining me for church tomorrow."

David watched Jenny squirm in her chair—*actually squirm*—and fought the urge to laugh.

It was fleeting, however, when Estelle turned her attention on him, her brow further wrinkled by a frown of concern.

"They told us you're about to lose your business."

Something akin to shame shot through him, as Jenny turned surprised and troubled eyes on him.

Emotions churned. He couldn't lambaste his pastor for betraying him when *had* mentioned the problem to Liam, asked him to keep his eyes and ears open and had not specified that it was a confidential matter.

But the last thing he wanted was Jenny knowing that things with him hadn't been just fine since she left.

Chapter Eight

The last thing David Hart would ever want was to have his business—personal or otherwise—discussed during a luncheon at the pastor's house. Jenny knew this as surely as she knew that the sun rose every morning.

She also knew that the best thing to do was to distract Gran, change the subject and gracefully steer the conversation in another direction. Yet somehow, the next words out of her mouth were "You're losing your business?"

Then she saw Reba standing in the kitchen door. "You're losing your business, Dad?"

He beckoned her over, exquisitely gentle with her, even though Jenny knew how difficult a spot he was in.

"No, sweetheart, I'm not losing my business. I'm just looking for a new office location."

He said the words lightly enough, but Jenny could still read all too well the lines of worry etched on his face.

David stroked Reba's cheek. "Aren't you supposed to be resting? Where's your sister?"

Reba shrugged. "I felt better after I lay down for a few minutes. But Rowe fell asleep."

"Well, there's a switch," David murmured. "So what would you like to do? Listen to boring grown-up talk or play a game of checkers?"

"Checkers!" Reba proclaimed.

"Good choice," David said.

Jenny's heart tugged at what a good father he was, lifting any weight he could off his girls' young shoulders, even when he had his own heavy load to carry.

"Estelle," he said, "I'm glad to hear you enjoyed your lunch. Do you still keep the board games in the same spot?" Estelle nodded and started to rise from her chair. "No, don't get up. I can find them."

After David and Reba had gone to start their game of checkers, Jenny said, "I'm sorry that you didn't finish telling us about your lunch visit."

Estelle smiled. "Lunch was delicious," she said. "We had egg salad sandwiches. You know, hardly anyone knows how to make a good egg salad sandwich anymore. The secret is that…"

This time, instead of trying to steer the conversation, Jenny let her grandma chatter contentedly on about the right ratio of mayonnaise to egg, and how finely one should chop the green onions, while her thoughts whirled around the possible repercussions of David's predicament.

He had sounded casual enough, obviously not wanting to trouble Reba, but she knew him better than that. She also knew that it wasn't easy to find premium office space, so what better place than her grandmother's house? It was spacious enough to allow room for an office, without interfering with the living space of the house. In fact, her grandpa's den, a room that her grandma had barely touched since he had passed away, might be perfect.

Maybe she could offer David that as office space—not that it was hers to offer.

"Jenny, are you listening?" Her grandma's rather petulant-sounding voice broke into her churning thoughts.

"I'm sorry, Gran. I'm—what do you call it? Wool-gathering?"

"I asked if you wanted more tea."

"Oh. No, thanks, I'm good."

"Well, I could use some myself, not that anyone is asking."

Jenny smiled in apology and picked up the teapot to refill her grandmother's cup, then decided, after all, to top up her own.

"Gran?" she asked, lowering her voice cautiously, "what else did they say about David's business?"

Gran's eyes turned suddenly sharp. "Now, Jenny, you know I don't like gossip. Nothing good was ever accomplished by gossiping."

"I wasn't—" Jenny started to protest but then closed her mouth and took a sip of tea instead. Gran was certainly right about one thing: it wouldn't do any good to hear the details of David's situation. His troubles, whatever they may be, were his to work out, and he didn't need or want her to be part of the solution, even if she could be.

Rowena appeared in the kitchen just then, looking slightly disheveled and seemed grumpy. Jenny thought she also looked younger and more vulnerable, and her heart went out to the girl, whose tough shell and challenging behavior signaled a need to be reassured that she was still worth paying attention to.

"Hi, Rowe," she said brightly. "Would you like something to drink?"

Rowe shook her head and folded her arms across her chest. "Where's my dad and Reba?|"

"Playing checkers. Come on, I'll help you find them."

Rowe wrinkled her nose. "We musta played checkers and stuff for like a billion hours in the hospital. I thought we were going to do fun stuff here."

"Rowe? I thought I heard your voice." David walked into the kitchen. "Come with me. If you don't want to play checkers with us, I'm sure we can find something else to do that we'll all enjoy. You don't need to be bothering Jenny."

"She's not bothering me," Jenny protested, but David had already turned to exit the room, and after a moment's hesitation, Rowena followed him.

A little while later, Jenny helped Gran settle in her room for a nap, and then craving fresh air, she put on her light blue winter coat and her snow boots to head out for a walk.

She cautiously touched the steps with her foot before walking down them and was cautious for the first few steps before hitting her stride once she was on the sidewalk. In her travels abroad, Jenny had learned that people tended to think that Saskatchewan suffered through deep-freeze temperatures for most of the year. But, even in January, the weather could fluctuate wildly from melting to freezing, sometimes even a rain shower thrown in for good measure, so she was always aware that there could be unexpected icy patches under the snow. A good pair of boots helped, or grippers if it was especially slippery, but mostly it was important to stay aware and know where your feet were landing.

She needed to know where she was going to land in more ways than one.

Jenny walked to the end of the block and turned left onto Central Street, which was the bustling heart of Living Skies.

Of course, Jenny had already been into Graham's Grocers and other stores earlier that day for Christmas treats, but she had been greeted by people she hadn't seen for a long time and was self-conscious and all too aware of being there with David and his daughters.

Now, she stood at the corner for a moment to take it all in, and nostalgia slammed over her in waves. A walk down Central Street would be, she knew, an unrelenting walk into her past: Murphy's restaurant, where she and David had shared countless burgers and fries and tall glasses of chocolate milkshakes; Debra's Delightful Designs, where she bought dresses for school dances and other special occasions; Hart's Hardware that David's father owned and, from what she gathered, showed no sign of retiring from; the office that housed the *Living Skies Chronicle*…

Jenny walked toward the newspaper's office, half expecting it not to be open on a Saturday, even though the former editor declined to shut its door for anything other than what he called in his gruff but genuine way *the Lord's day.*

But when she got there, it was clear that the office was open.

Gran's oft-repeated phrase that God helps those who help themselves came to Jenny's mind. If she was going to stay in Living Skies, she needed to find work, so why not start by asking at a place where she might get to do something that she actually wanted to do?

She had no good answer for why she had stopped writing, especially since that was one of the reasons she had given herself for her abrupt departure, other than it had been so easy to get caught up in meeting people, seeing sights and grabbing jobs here and there to make just enough money to make it to her next destination.

Besides, sitting down to write had meant thinking—and remembering—and that was something she couldn't allow herself to do.

She lifted her head, taking in deep breaths of frosty air. It made her eyes water with the cold, but that was better than giving in to emotional tears.

When Jenny opened the door of the *Chronicle*, it smelled just the way she remembered it: paper and dust and cedar. For an instant, she was a high-school girl again, dropping in to discuss writing and journalism with intrepid journalist Stew Wagner.

Of course, she reminded herself, Stew had retired a few years back. Grace had emailed her photos of his retirement party. Jenny had regretted not being able to be there, but something—some sense that if she slowed down, life would swallow her whole—had kept her from coming back to Living Skies, even for a visit.

The woman who came forward to greet her had short-cropped brown hair and inquisitive brown eyes. She was dressed in beige pants and a red sweater. She looked vaguely familiar but Jenny couldn't immediately place her.

"Jenny Powell?" the woman asked, her businesslike demeanor immediately dropping away.

"Natalie!" Jenny stepped forward and spontaneously hugged the other woman. Natalie Surasik had been a senior and editor of the school yearbook when Jenny was a freshman, full of more ideas than experience but determined to help out. Natalie had been a forthright but encouraging mentor.

She also, as Jenny recalled now, was someone who was willing to do almost anything to land a story.

"Did I catch you at a busy time?" Jenny asked, her shoulders arched and her hands wrung in sudden shyness.

"Unfortunately not," Natalie said. "Everyone seems to be reading their news online these days, and it can be tough to find a hook that makes them want to subscribe to a traditionally published paper. But it's great to see you. What brings you by? No, wait. I'll make us some coffee. Is instant okay?"

"That's good with me," Jenny said. "I'll take a splash of milk if you have it, but it's fine if you don't."

"I'll go rummage," Natalie said, "Grab a chair."

But feeling restless, instead of sitting down Jenny walked over to study a series of framed photographs on one of the walls: close-ups of people's faces with eyes that told haunting stories; athletes caught in poses that made the possibilities of the human body seem limitless; a variety of animals—bears with magnificent snarling faces, deer leaping with exquisite grace; and more.

They had not been there back when Stew was editor. She would not have forgotten photographs like that. But she didn't know any of the people, and there wasn't that kind of wildlife anywhere close to Living Skies, although you could see some if you drove about five hours farther north.

"Here you go," Natalie came up beside Jenny and handed her a mug of coffee. The mug read *Life is a story. Make yours a bestseller.*

"Thank you," Jenny said with her eyes still on the photos. "Are these from a magazine?"

"No," Natalie said. "These are John Bishop's. His family lived here for just a few years after you moved away. He was a highly talented photographer, as you can see. *Is*," she corrected herself. "*Is* a highly talented photographer. But he's rarely back in town anymore, though he does keep in touch and sends us copies of his work. There's not much to keep people in Living Skies. I guess you can relate to that."

She paused and sipped her coffee. "I keep telling myself I'm going to be the one to restore the paper to its former glory days. I just need stories that are really going to grab people so the subscription rates don't drop off any more than they have."

Jenny smiled nervously. "Actually," she said, as she took a chair beside the desk where Natalie plunked down her mug and sat down. "I'm back to stay, which is what I wanted to talk to you about."

"To stay?" Natalie's brows immediately scrunched in a way that reminded Jenny of how she had looked under pressing deadlines, or trying to sort the details of a tough story. Her desk still had the same organized clutter look to it. To anyone else it would look utterly chaotic, but Natalie would know where everything she needed was.

"Yes," Jenny hoped that the firmness in her voice would belie the trembling inside her. "You've probably heard that my grandmother isn't doing all that well."

"I have heard that," Natalie confirmed.

"I'm looking for work," Jenny said. *Might as well get right to the point.* "You always thought I was a good writer, and maybe I could help come up with some of those stories that would keep people interested."

"You're asking me if I would hire you as a writer?" The eyebrow scrunch was back. "I'm not really in a position to hire, but I suppose I could look at samples of your work," Natalie said. "Maybe run an article or two, but there's nothing full-time."

"I, uh, don't really have any recent samples." Jenny swallowed, and her nerves did a frantic dance. "I didn't have time to write…" She paused and made herself be honest. "I didn't make time to write while I traveled. There were just so many other things to do."

The excuse sounded weak even to her.

"That's too bad," Natalie said. "From what I recall, you did have talent." She took another sip of her coffee. Jenny's hand curled around her own mug, but had no interest for what was inside.

Natalie set her mug down and leaned forward, folding her hands. "Look, Jenny, if you need a job, there must be work at Murphy's or one of the shops. I could maybe even find you some odd jobs to do around here, but you must know I wouldn't hire a writer with no proven experience, even if I was in a position to do so."

Jenny nodded and forced a smile. "Can't blame a girl for trying."

"You always did have gumption, I'll give you that," Natalie said. "Listen," her eyes narrowed speculatively. "If you wanted to try writing a feature on spec, we could see where it goes. Something with human interest. Readers always like that. You could find other work, even assist me here with some of the grunt work, and in time, we might be able to start featuring some of your stories."

Jenny took a deep breath, praying wordlessly on the inhale and exhale. "What kind of human interest?"

"David Hart," Natalie said.

Hearing his name caused Jenny's hand to jerk involuntarily, and a few drops of coffee sprayed. Thankfully, it wasn't piping hot.

"Oh, that's right," Natalie said, reading the signs like any good reporter would. "You two were quite the item back in the day, weren't you?"

Jenny couldn't find her voice to respond.

"Anyway," Natalie carried on, "think about it. He's a single dad with a daughter who fought cancer. How are they doing? What's getting them through? People love stories of strength and inspiration."

"David would never go for it," she croaked out.

"Maybe not," Natalie said briskly. "But asking would be a good place to start, especially if you're serious about writing for us."

"I'll think about it." But she was already sure that she wouldn't do it. She could never do that to David or to his daughters.

Jenny finished her coffee out of politeness and told Natalie a few anecdotes from her travels. Then she thanked Natalie for her time and said she would be in touch.

David would not let her write a story about him and especially not about Reba, not in a million years, she thought as she walked home, and she would never want to expose their vulnerabilities.

God, she prayed, *what am I supposed to do now?*

The flicker of disappointment on Reba's face told David that she had been enjoying some one-on-one time with him and had hoped that Rowe would stay asleep upstairs a bit longer.

Rowena, no doubt, thought that Reba had more than her share of time with him and perhaps couldn't, or didn't want to, understand that driving Reba for radiation and having her cling to his hand while he desperately tried to distract her from nausea with songs, stories and lame dad jokes didn't exactly count as quality time.

"Would you girls like to play a game together?" David asked, thinking he could use the time to make a couple of phone calls.

Reba's eyes darted to her twin's face and fell away when she saw only disinterest there.

"Can't we just finish our game, Daddy?" Her voice was on the brink of whining. She hadn't called him Daddy for a long time.

"Oh, just go ahead," Rowena said. She tucked her thick hair behind her ears. It fell in a blunt edge to her shoulders. "Where's Jenny? She'd probably do something fun with me while you play boring old checkers."

"I don't know where Jenny is," David said and suddenly had the sensation that he didn't like not knowing. "Maybe out for a walk. Estelle is resting, though, so whatever you decide to do, please do it quietly."

"So I'm stuck being bored like always." Rowe sighed dramatically.

Lord, I'm feeling overwhelmed here, David prayed silently, seeking the best way to respond to Rowe. *My daughters both need me, I need to find office space, Jenny needs—*

He interrupted his own prayer. What Jenny Powell

needed wasn't his business, much as he still had the urge to help her.

I need to help Estelle fix up this house, like I promised, he amended. *And, despite all of this, somehow I have to give my girls a merry Christmas. I'm trusting You, Lord, because I don't know how I'm going to do it all myself.*

There was a distant sound of the front door opening, and Rowe's face lit up with relief. "Jenny's back!" she cried as she ran from the room.

Reba picked up a checkers piece and wiggled it in her hand a little while wriggling in her chair at the same time.

"You can go see Jenny too if that's what you want," David said, resigned.

That was Jenny. People always loved to see her.

He briefly thought about continuing to hide out with the checkerboard but reminded himself that he was an adult, so he followed close behind them.

Jenny's cheeks were pink with cold, and the jacket she wore made her eyes even bluer. It must have started to snow a bit because frosty flakes adorned her pretty hair like tiny, glittering stars.

He looked away.

"Estelle is still resting in her room," he said by way of greeting.

"Oh, good. Thanks." She appeared distracted shrugging off her coat. It somehow got hung up on her arm and David stepped forward to help, then stopped himself from making physical contact, not trusting the way his emotions jumbled at the sight of the snowflakes in her hair.

"It's snowing?" Rowena ran to the front window and back again. "Can we go outside?"

Reba's eyes shone. "We could build a snowman," she suggested.

"I don't know if there's enough snow for a snowman," Jenny said, her eyes meeting David's as she slowly started to ease her jacket back on. "But, it might be fun to be outside, if that's okay with your dad?"

David nodded. "Sure, it would be good to get some fresh air. If we can't build a snowman, I'm sure that the lawn would be perfect for snow angels."

The twins whooped and scrambled to find their outdoor wear.

"I should look in on Gran," Jenny said. "Let her know what we're doing. Unless…you just want to be alone with your girls."

"No," David said, proud and somewhat amazed that his voice carried none of the weight of his thoughts. "You're the star attraction here. They're both excited you're back."

She looked at him with a question in her eyes.

"What?" he asked.

"I just wondered…"

But then the twins came running in, excited to get outside.

"I'll just leave a note for Gran," Jenny said. "I'll be right out."

Outside, the day was sunny and the air was crisp, and David found some respite in watching his daughters fall into the freshly fallen snow on the front lawn and move their arms and legs in the time-honored fashion of making snow angels.

He had better things to think about than how Jenny Powell looked with snow adorning her hair.

She plopped down in between his daughters to make her own angel but stumbled getting up and ruined hers, causing the girls to giggle. As she pretended to be angry and chase them around the yard, their laughter escalating into happy shrieks, David knew he hadn't seen them look that happy in a long time.

He couldn't dislike a woman who did that for his daughters, much as it would protect his heart to do so.

The following Sunday, David and the twins got ready for church. Although it wouldn't be true to say that he'd never had a doubt or question or angry moment at God—and still had them—during the ordeal with Reba's cancer and Cheryl's leaving, at his core he always knew that he wanted God to be an integral part of their lives.

Pastor Liam's passionate sermons at Good Shepherd Church always stirred him to strive to be a better person.

He was endlessly grateful for the congregation too. He didn't know how he would have made it through if it hadn't been for church members providing food and running errands, while he and the twins were adjusting to their new normal, and continuing to be there with ongoing prayers and shoulders to lean on.

He wondered if Jenny had found that kind of trusting bond with any congregations on her travels, but she hadn't looked all that keen when Estelle had reminded her that they would be attending church. It was hard to say, though, if that was a reflection of her spiritual state or reluctance to face more curiosity.

A memory passed through his mind of the times that he and Jenny had attended youth group together. One time they'd gone on a hayride and one of the kids hadn't bothered to tell the leaders that he was allergic to hay and so...

David gave his head a quick, sharp shake. Even if Jenny Powell was part of almost every memory he had in Living Skies, that didn't mean he had to dwell on them.

He went to wake up Reba and Rowe.

Standing in the doorway of the bedroom, David took a moment to drink in the sight of his sleeping daughters and, as he did every morning, said a prayer.

He always marveled at how the way they slept was completely opposite to their personalities. Rowena lay on her back, the covers barely rumpled, her mouth turned upward in a perpetual, small smile as if life was good and she hadn't a care in the world. It was Reba who turned the sheets and blankets into tangled disarray, while her face wore an expression of petulant annoyance as if she could no longer be bothered to hold in the burdens that plagued her throughout her days.

He wished he could truly know their thoughts.

Maybe he had spent too much time praising Reba for being brave and keeping her chin up. Maybe what he should have done—and still be doing—was tell her to scream and cry and be afraid because she was only eight years old and had been forced to fight off a disease that many who were older and stronger than her had succumbed to.

Jenny would know.

Of course, he had known too. He had seen her through it all: the moments of victory and the moments of despair.

Enjoying Your Book?

Start saving on new books like the one you're reading with the *Harlequin Reader Service!*

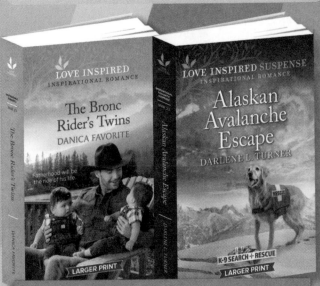

Get Free Books In Just 3 Easy Steps

Are you an avid reader searching for more books?
The **Harlequin Reader Service** might be for you! We'd love to send you up to **4 free books** just for trying it out. Just write **"YES"** on the **Free Books Voucher Card** and we'll send your free books and a gift, altogether worth over $20.

Step 1: Choose your Books

Try *Love Inspired® Romance Larger-Print* and get 2 books and fall in love with inspirational romances that take you on an uplifting journey of faith, forgiveness and hope.

Try *Love Inspired® Suspense Larger-Print* and get 2 books where courage and optimism unite in stories of faith and love in the face of danger.

Or *TRY BOTH!*

Step 2: Return your completed Free Books Voucher Card

Step 3: Receive your books and continue reading!

Your free books are **completely free**, even the shipping! If you continue with your subscription, you can look forward to curated monthly shipments of brand-new books from your selected series, always at a discount off the cover price! Plus you can cancel any time.

Don't miss out, reply today! Over $20 FREE value.

Free Books Voucher Card

YES! I love reading, please send me more books from the series I'd like to explore and a free gift from each series I select.

More books are just 3 steps away!

Just write in "**YES**" on the dotted line below then select your series and return this Books Voucher today and we'll send your free books & a gift asap!

 YES

Choose your books:

☐ **Love Inspired®** **Romance** **Larger-Print** 122/322 CTI G29D	☐ **Love Inspired®** **Suspense** **Larger-Print** 107/307 CTI G29D	☐ **BOTH** 122/322 & 107/307 CTI G29F

FIRST NAME

LAST NAME

ADDRESS

APT.#

CITY

STATE/PROV.

ZIP/POSTAL CODE

EMAIL ☐ Please check this box if you would like to receive newsletters and promotional emails from Harlequin Enterprises ULC and its affiliates. You can unsubscribe anytime.

LI/LIS-1123-OM_123ST

The memories were too troubling, so he buried them in a quick prayer that the Lord would guide their days.

It didn't take long after the girls were awake for their sleep personalities to fall away and be replaced by what David expected to see. Reba went immediately into the bathroom to splash water on her sleepy face and brush her teeth, while Rowe grumbled something about hating church, which wasn't true—she was just grouchy when she first woke up—and folded the pillow in half to make a sandwich of her head.

But, in a reasonably short period of time, they both appeared at the breakfast table with their hair neatly brushed and their faces looking pink from recent washing. Both wore navy blue pants, but Reba wore a pale pink turtleneck with hers, while Rowe's light blue cardigan swung open over a blue-and-white checked blouse.

"Good job," David praised automatically, but he couldn't stop his eyes from gravitating toward where Jenny sat at the kitchen table with her grandma.

Thankfully his daughters were busy getting settled into their chairs and reaching for the cereal boxes that had been set out on the table, because he didn't want them to catch him staring at Jenny like a starstruck schoolboy.

Because, despite all the still very real reasons he had for not letting his heart get tangled with hers again, there had always had been and always would be something about her fresh beauty that captivated him.

For church, she had her hair pulled up into a loose knot that emphasized her cheekbones, and the periwinkle knit dress she wore brought out her blue eyes and was a flattering style for her tall, slim shape.

But, as attracted as he might always be to her, he would never allow himself to go down that road again. Because knowing how it was bound to end simply hurt too much.

Chapter Nine

David Hart had definitely grown into a handsome man.

Growing up, he had been appealing in a boyishly cute, slightly awkward way. But now that awkwardness was completely gone, and seeing him in his black pants and maroon dress shirt for church made her breath catch a bit, especially with his eyes probing hers.

She wished she could get up the courage to talk to him about the potential article. She wouldn't write the kind of exploitive piece she sensed Natalie was going for, but maybe David could help her come up with... *something*.

"Is there something wrong?" David asked. "You're looking at me funny."

"No," Jenny shook her head, as she felt her face grow warm. "No." Then she gathered her courage and said all in a rush, "But I would like you ask you about something."

"Oh? Okay, just let me know when you're ready."

In those words was a glimpse of practical, patient David from her past, and Jenny took heart in that.

The moment Jenny stepped into Good Shepherd

Church, it was like stepping into a time capsule, and the familiar sights and smells smoothed away her jitters.

During her years away, she had visited many churches but hadn't become attached to any. There wasn't any point. She had been everywhere from plain, modest buildings to services that were held in former sports arenas. But Good Shepherd, with its dark wood pews and stained glass windows and the scent of candles burning and the organ piping out "Holy, Holy, Holy!" would always be the definition of church to her.

They found a pew, and David and Jenny ended up sitting at opposite ends, which was probably just as well, she thought.

But memories stirred of them sitting together, his knee nudging hers, him leaning over to whisper something in her ear—sometimes something genuine about the sermon, sometimes an attempt to make her laugh.

"As you know, Pastor Liam and his wife won't be with us today," said Bill Russell, who was making the announcements after the opening hymn and prayer, "as they've gone to visit his aunt in Winnipeg. She's just had hip surgery so we send our prayers for her healing and their safe travels."

Jenny slid a sideways glance toward her grandmother, who sat beside her, wearing one of her favorite dresses for church, a long-sleeved deep purple dress with a flouncy skirt that would perhaps have been more suited to a younger woman but was somehow charming on her.

Gran hadn't said anything about Pastor Liam not giving the sermon today, and Jenny couldn't help wondering if they had mentioned it at lunch yesterday and Gran didn't recall.

"Please stand, as you're able, for the gospel reading."

"That's Sam Meyer, the new associate pastor," Gran whispered in explanation. "I'm sure he'll preach well."

Jenny studied him. Sam was slightly stocky and had warm hazel eyes. His face was serious but lit up as soon as he started speaking. As Gran predicted, he delivered an engrossing sermon.

After the service, people milled around chatting in the church foyer, enjoying the cookies and coffee that were put out, along with apple juice for the kids.

Jenny noticed Nancy Chamberlain with her little boy, who was kicking up a fuss, and her husband, and she was relieved when they went straight to the coatrack to make a hasty exit.

She did smile and wave at Grace, though. She welcomed a chat with her friend but, at the same time, wanted to keep an eye out for David and for an opportunity to chat. And, as was expected, others came over to say hello and catch up too. Jenny knew she couldn't escape after church without facing greetings and questions.

She kept her smile on and stuck to a couple of her favorite travel anecdotes.

In the meantime, Gran had wandered over to a table that held a tray of shortbread—her favorite—and was selecting one, while answering something that Vivian Russell said, smiling her thanks as Vivian poured her a cup of coffee.

Gran was truly loved in the congregation, and it gave Jenny some sense of relief to know that her grandma had friends. Still, as family, ultimately the responsibility for Gran's future care was in her hands. Of course, her parents were part of it too, at least in theory. Their frequent missions meant they would not be at the center of Gran's care, and Jenny didn't expect that to change.

Then her stomach jolted in dismay when she realized again that despite her unmistakable signs of aging, Gran had her life and her friends here and had managed without Jenny for years. It was Jenny who had no roots, no job, no real place to call home.

Then she saw David. He had one hand on the shoulder of each of his daughters and was chatting with Pastor Sam.

Jenny watched the serious-looking young pastor suddenly throw his head back and laugh, and she was regretfully reminded that it was only with her that David had become distant. With others, he was still warm and engaging, someone people were drawn to and instinctively trusted.

She was jealous. She knew it was wrong, but she was.

She was also disappointed, but mostly in herself. She knew—or at least had known—David well enough to know that he was devastated by her leaving but might have been consoled by telling himself that at least she had left to pursue her dreams.

But she hadn't done that, so what exactly *had* she done with her life, and what was her future going to look like?

She watched David, who appeared to be wrapping up his conversation with the pastor. She could tell by Rowena's body language that she was getting restless and soon it would be lunchtime. She wanted to have the conversation with him about her writing an article before other conversations took over.

She wondered if there was any possible way she

could write an article that would appeal to Natalie without offending him.

Jenny lifted her chin and squared her shoulders. If David was disappointed or hurt that she hadn't made it as a writer, didn't that give her even more reason to write a compelling article?

She had faced opponents on the basketball and volleyball courts; she had taken care of herself through several years of travel; she had stood up to a dishonest boss, even though it had cost her job—surely she could face David honestly and ask for what she wanted.

David and Pastor Sam parted ways with a handshake and another laugh, then David nodded at something Reba said, and the twins scooted off to grab a cookie each, while he headed off to get their coats.

Gran was still engrossed in conversation; she was, in fact, blocking access to the coffeepot, but everyone appeared to be patient with her. Once again, Jenny was grateful that her grandmother had such an understanding church home.

David had his coat on and was helping Reba with the zipper on her coat while Rowe tugged at her own.

Never had Jenny wanted more to be two people at the same time. She needed to catch up with David, but she wanted to make sure Gran would be attended to as well. Her eyes rapidly scanned the room.

Spotting Grace, Jenny called her over and quickly explained the situation.

"Sure, I'll chat with Estelle until you get back," Grace agreed easily.

Jenny thanked her and hurried over to find her own coat. She put it on as quickly as she could and rushed outside where David and the girls were just at the end of the front walk.

"David!" she called.

When he turned his puzzled face to her, she was a bit embarrassed at her franticness. They were going back to the same place, but her need to get the conversation over with was now like something hot churning in her stomach.

She caught up with him. "Could I have a private word?" she asked. "It won't take long."

The hesitation was plain on David's face, but he indicated the girls should wait for him a few steps away. As she began to speak, Jenny saw Reba tugging nervously at the end of her scarf, while Rowe made no secret of glaring at them.

As succinctly as she could, Jenny told David about her spontaneous meeting with Natalie at the *Chronicle* and how she might have the chance to get a job there—a real writing job!—if she could turn in a human-interest story that would catch everybody's attention.

As she had always done, to quell the doubts and fears that always wanted to crawl out from the inner recesses to ask why her parents cared so much about helping others that they were willing to leave her behind, Jenny dug deep for self-assurance.

As she spoke, she gained confidence. David knew her well enough to know that she would treat the subject with tact and sensitivity

She wrapped up her pitch with a hopeful smile and an inward prayer.

"Not a chance," David said.

"But…"

David's eyes darted over to the girls—Reba had

stopped any pretense of preoccupying herself—and Jenny knew it was only for their sake that he controlled his reaction.

David didn't really have a temper: he preferred to get along with people and to keep things on a positive note. But he wasn't a pushover either, and if you tried to shove him off the hill he was willing to die on, he would anchor himself and stand strong.

"I really can't believe you would ask me that," he shook his head incredulously. "You take off without a word, except that letter. I don't hear from you for years, then you show up again out of the blue, and now you decide you want to jump-start your long-neglected writing career by exploiting my daughter?"

"I wouldn't exploit her," Jenny spluttered, trying to keep calm as David's anger escalated. "David, you know me better than that."

"Do I?" He shook his head. "I'm not sure I do anymore, not at all."

Hurt and frustration mingled bitterly in the back of Jenny's throat. She struggled to find words to defend herself and present her case in a way that he would understand, but David shook his head, his face like granite.

"I don't want to discuss this anymore, and I'm thinking it's probably best if we make other arrangements for a place to stay while they finish the work at our house."

"Dad!"

Further regret ate at Jenny's insides as she realized that, in letting her frustration get the better of her, she had momentarily forgotten that the girls were even there.

Both David and she turned to look where Rowe

pointed and saw that Reba was standing there shaking and gasping as tears poured down her face.

Dear God, please help, David prayed silently but frantically as he fled toward his daughter.

"What's wrong?" He knelt in front of Reba, unmindful of the snow.

"I-I do-don't want to leave Christ-Christmas House!" Reba stuttered out between sobs. "It's no-no f-fun at home."

All the thoughts that David was having about what could be physically wrong with his daughter—he was already mentally scheduling a barrage of hospital visits—slammed together like a multicar pileup.

So, there was nothing physically wrong with her. *Thank You, Lord.* But initial relief was mixed with a barrage of other emotions. There were simply too many other things to contend with, including the fact that being around Jenny caused such a roller coaster within him that he acted in ways that he didn't want his daughters exposed to.

His daughters, he thought with a sigh. If gentle, agreeable Reba was this upset, Rowe would be fit to be tied.

He still had one arm around Reba, and he rummaged in his pocket and found a crumpled but clean tissue and helped her blow her nose into it. At the same time, his eyes sought Rowena.

How many times since Cheryl left had he wished that he could be two people? He loved both of his daughters equally and endlessly but perpetually struggled with the even distribution of his attention. It often seemed impossible to be fair and balanced.

But now Rowe was engaged in deep conversation with Jenny.

Jenny squatted beside his daughter and held both of her mittened hands in her own. David knew well the expression of grave attentiveness on Jenny's face as Rowe earnestly poured out whatever was on her mind.

As impulsive and stubborn as she could be, David knew that there was no better listener than Jenny Powell. He swallowed a lump made up of strongly conflicted emotions at the sight of Rowe discovering the same.

As if sensing his gaze on them, Jenny lifted her face. The call to battle had left her face, but there were still many questions there.

"I have to get Gran," she said, quietly. "I asked Grace to keep her company, and she'll be wondering where I am."

She added something to Rowe that David couldn't hear and squeezed her hands before standing up. Rowe nodded and came over to join him and Reba.

"What were you and Jenny talking about?" David couldn't resist asking Rowe as Jenny headed back into the church to get her grandmother. He assumed Jenny wouldn't be any more eager to walk home together than he was, so he and the girls started back to the house. Reba was still snuffling.

Maybe he should put some pressure on Bruce to speed up with the hopes that once they were back in their own house, they would all realize that it was still their home.

And maybe all of his other problems would suddenly sprout wings and fly away...

David sighed. Pushing away his own thoughts, he realized that Rowena was uncharacteristically quiet.

"What did you and Jenny talk about?" he asked again, slightly more insistent.

Rowe shrugged and addressed her boots. "Just that you really love us and stuff."

David's insides twisted in an unexpected way at the words. As always his emotions were conflicted when it came to Jenny having any part in their lives. Part of him was glad that Rowe had listened to Jenny and had been able to talk to her, but there was still a greater part of him who didn't exactly want his daughter confiding in the woman who had left him.

During lunch, which was an awkward, polite affair, while Estelle was blissfully unaware of any tension, she recounted the sermon and gave her views on it.

It was interesting, David thought, that she could manage to do that with admirable accuracy but couldn't grasp that he and Jenny weren't a couple anymore, and maybe not even friends.

But, despite some apprehension about it, he kept remembering Jenny talking to Rowe and how Rowe, who had been like a small, brittle leaf blown everywhere by the winds of things she couldn't control, had been still and calm.

And despite their frustration with each other, she had chosen to say what Rowena needed to hear the most: he loved them.

He thoughtfully spooned up the last of the chicken noodle soup in his bowl and wondered if there was a way they could live compatibly until his home repairs were done.

The last thing they needed was another upheaval in their lives.

To lay the foundation to a smoother path, David offered to clean up the kitchen while Jenny attended to Estelle, who was ready for an afternoon rest.

Jenny raised her eyebrows momentarily, then nodded. "Thank you."

David dismissed the girls too. Rowena was still subdued as if still pondering her talk with Jenny, and Reba was showing the physical effects of an emotional upheaval, her eyes heavy and her skin pale, but thankfully her breathing was regular, and he was confident some quiet time would eliminate the other symptoms. In any case, both of the girls went willingly to their room, which was a good thing because he needed time to sort out his thoughts.

As he stacked the dishes into the sink and wiped the table, stovetop and countertops free of crumbs and splashes, David considered what it would take to put his lingering resentments aside and provide his girls the Christmas he had promised.

Because the thing he couldn't allow himself to forget, however he felt about everything else, was that he *had* promised them. He had to stop acting like a boy with hurt feelings.

Even if the pain still ran through his veins.

Okay, he would call a truce, he half decided, half prayed for help. But the article still had to be a no-go. Among many reasons, he could only imagine his daughters' reactions to having Reba's cancer battle brought front and center again, and it wasn't good.

He was drying the last bowl when Jenny poked her head into the kitchen. The cautious expression on her face made his heart stagger.

I really have been acting like a jerk.

"It looks great in here," she commented.

"I always was better at tidying up than you were."

It was an acknowledgment of their shared past, a small olive branch, and for a moment an uneasy expression flickered across Jenny's face, but then she smiled

"That you were." There was a beat of silence, and then she added, "I want to" just as David was saying, "I think we should…"

"You go," Jenny gestured to one of the kitchen chairs, then held up the coffeepot with a questioning look.

David hesitated then nodded. Maybe it would be easier to say what was on his mind if she was doing something else while she listened instead of staring him down with those cornflower blue eyes.

So while Jenny poured water into the coffee maker, measured out scoops of ground coffee and got mugs out of the cupboard, he decided to get one of the biggest elephants out of the way first.

"I hate not getting along with you, Jen." As he said it, David saw Jenny go still, the hand holding a teaspoon of sugar above a cup of coffee paused in midair.

"I don't like it either," she said, resuming her action after a moment.

"I especially don't want us to ever quarrel again in front of the girls," David continued. "They got enough of that with…well, when things weren't good with Cheryl and me."

Jenny bit her lip but remained silent. She opened the fridge and splashed some milk into the same mug she'd put the sugar in and came over to the table to hand it to him.

So, she knew that he still liked his coffee with a spoonful of sugar and milk, not cream.

While he was preparing what he was going to say,

Jenny leaped up and returned with a plate of store-bought oatmeal chocolate chip cookies.

"Dessert," she proclaimed.

David smiled a wistful smile, while memories like the last, lingering notes of a once-familiar song whispered through him. They must have eaten hundreds of these cookies over the years, first with milk and then, as they grew up, with tea or coffee.

Jenny didn't appear to notice the impact the gesture had on him. She dunked a cookie into her coffee—something about the action made her look like she was about twelve years old again, despite the coffee—and after she had chewed and swallowed asked, "What did you and Cheryl quarrel about?"

Then she immediately clapped a hand over her mouth. That was something she used to do in jest, after she had knowingly provoked him with some comment. David could still remember her eyes dancing with laughter over those hands that pretended to be contrite.

Except this time there was no laughter in those eyes.

Jenny slowly lowered her hand. "I'm so sorry," she said. "That is absolutely none of my business."

"It's okay," David said.

Maybe it was because, however deep it was buried, there was still a part of him that told Jenny Powell everything, or maybe it was because there wasn't really anyone else in Living Skies that he wanted to confide in. Whatever the reason, David said, "I used to think it was mostly about how she couldn't handle Reba being sick—I mean, in some ways, I wasn't even all that surprised when she left—but the truth is, I don't think Cheryl and I ever really wanted the same things."

Jenny nodded slowly, her eyes met his. She'd always

had that way of looking at him not like she was trying to find out his secrets but like she would always be understanding if he chose to share them.

But, Lord, I don't know if I can trust her anymore.

But he knew he would only find that out by giving it a try.

Steam curled out of the coffee mug. David blew gently on the hot beverage. Jenny had finished her cookie but didn't reach for another one. His remained untouched on his plate.

The house was quiet, but he doubted it would be for long. They might not get another chance to hash things out.

"You didn't know Cheryl," David began. "She's from Regina. I met her after you'd left. She was working at Debra's clothing store for the summer."

Jenny nodded, as if she had heard as much from the town grapevine.

"What else do you know about Cheryl?" David asked. There was no point going into a lot of detail if he was just repeating things. Of course, no one knew what went on behind the scenes—the quick flashes of her temper, the long, petulant silences—and Cheryl was an attractive, outgoing woman, never more in her element than when she was the center of attention.

And it wasn't possible for her to be that when Reba got cancer.

David tamped the thought down. It was a dreadful and complicated thing to be the parent of a sick child, and no one had the right to judge…not even the other parent.

Despite Cheryl's flaws and his awareness that he had plenty of his own, he would never have willingly ended the marriage. People were meant to marry for life. He still believed that.

No matter how much evidence there was to the contrary.

"I don't really know much at all," Jenny answered him.

"She was a fun person, very sociable, a good mom," David said, doing his best to bring out some good qualities about his ex-wife. Dragging her down in a verbal assault wouldn't do any of them any good, and it certainly wouldn't change anything. "Reba's illness was just…it was very hard on her."

Jenny nodded. "It must have been so difficult for her…for both of you."

Her eyes were full of genuine sorrow. She had always been empathetic, taking on the emotions of others as if they were her own.

David added, almost in spite of himself, "You and she are pretty much complete opposites."

Jenny gave him a questioning look.

"I don't mean that you're not outgoing too." He squirmed like a floundering fish on the beach. "It's just…different."

David paused, then picked up a cookie. Studied it and put it down again. His stomach was in a jumble. His coffee grew cold.

"You're a good person, Jenny," he added softly.

Her eyes shone at him over her own mug as she took a sip.

He had loved two very different women, David pondered, and they had both chosen to leave him. But, if he was being brutally honest, he would have to say that Jenny had never exhibited the kind of moodiness or self-absorption that Cheryl had during their marriage.

So, did that mean that Jenny had left Living Skies not to hurt him but to find herself?

He didn't know, but when he looked at the face he had loved for so many years, he found himself willing to consider it.

Chapter Ten

For a moment Jenny allowed the fond memories that David's statement had evoked wash over her.

Just a few days before her fifteenth birthday, they were walking home from a picnic in the park, joking and play shoving, their elbows jostling the way they always did. Then their arms touched, the way they had done hundreds of times before, but David suddenly went still.

"What's wrong?" she had asked.

He had turned to her—she remembered it being almost like it was in slow motion—and had looked at her with intensity in his deep brown eyes that she had never seen before.

"I think I like you more than anyone I've ever known, Jenny Powell," he had said.

And after that, nothing was the same between them.

David cleared his throat. There was no intensity in his eyes now, just the kind of question that made Jenny's cheeks flush wondering if she'd looked like she was about to swoon.

She snapped herself back into the present moment, and David's expression that said that he already regretted that moment of softness was a clear reminder that those days were long gone.

As if also remembering that, David straightened up in his chair and with a businesslike posture said, "About that article, I hope you understand—"

"I'm not going to write the article," Jenny said, a bone-deep weariness creeping through her, as she wondered what she *was* going to do. "I understand what you said, and I respect it."

David's shoulders relaxed slightly and leaned back in his chair.

He picked up a cookie, took a bite and chewed thoughtfully, then grimaced slightly.

"What's wrong?" Jenny asked.

"Nothing…except we really used to love these, didn't we?" He picked up what remained of the cookie and studied it like it was some kind of newly discovered specimen. "Apparently, we didn't have very high standards back in the day."

"Are you kidding, Hart?" Jenny asked, feigning shock. "I still love them!" To prove her point she took a huge bite out of one of her cookies, then had to chew slowly and carefully, to make sure she didn't choke.

"Nice." David nodded deadpan. "Your manners are impeccable as always, Powell."

She managed to swallow before laughter overtook her, and David joined in.

Then, they both quickly sobered, and their eyes met.

Dear Lord, please help me find the words, Jenny silently prayed.

"Truce?" was what came out.

It was a simple word. It didn't say nearly what she wanted it to say, but at the same time, it said everything.

"I just don't know if it's that easy anymore," David said, as his deep brown eyes carried memories and regret that showed that he did remember.

"I'm not saying it's ever going to be like it used to be," Jenny said. "Or that's even what we want. But it's the Christmas season, David. We both have our reasons for being here. Can't we just do what we said we were going to do and enjoy the season, and help everyone else to enjoy it too?"

David nodded slowly. "We can try."

He picked up his coffee mug, studied the contents briefly, and set it back down again.

"Why didn't you write, Jen?" David's almost stern expression was counteracted by him using her shortened name.

Jenny recalled how they had once shared so many dreams with each other, shared them so intensely and without barriers that they had become intertwined, and it had been hard to know where one of their goals ended and the other began.

David had wanted her to succeed almost more than she did.

She shrugged helplessly. She could hardly explain it to herself, let alone him. She never wanted to play the cancer card—especially not with David, who had become a member of the club no one wanted to belong to, but sometimes there was no other way to try to explain something.

"I meant to. Honestly, I did," Jenny said. The cookie that she had gobbled down to give them a moment of levity now sat like a stone in her stomach. "I kept thinking I would get back to pursuing my writing goals. But, at first, it was just enough to know I had beat cancer,

I was free to figure out what I wanted to do with my writing—with my life.

She stopped and grimaced, knowing that David must be thinking that one of the first options she had chosen was to leave him behind.

She didn't look at him: she didn't want to see his expression.

"I didn't leave *you*. I left…" But how could she explain that what she had tried to leave was the fear that life would always hold more than she could accomplish or have time for, because in doing that, she *had* left him, no matter how she tried to spin it.

"Anyway," she rushed to say something that poorly resembled an answer, "I caught the travel bug. I needed money to travel, and life got to be a cycle of taking what jobs I could and earning enough money so that I could travel again."

"What's happened to that travel bug now?" David asked, quietly. "Was this really the first time you were worried enough about Estelle to come home?"

Jenny dared to look at David. There was nothing confrontational in his steady gaze, just genuine curiosity

But she didn't want to tell him that she'd lost her last job, and she didn't want to give him a reason to think that her reasons for returning home were self-serving.

Because they weren't.

At least, not entirely.

"I'm concerned for Gran all the time, and I always have been." She refused to sound defensive. "I just knew in my heart it was the right time to come home."

David's mouth tightened as he gave a brief nod. He picked up his plate and cup and stood.

"I should go check on the girls."

Jenny nodded, partly disappointed and partly re-lieved that their conversation had drawn to a close. They had made some headway, but she was still steer-ing carefully around many potential obstacles.

Would there ever be a time when David Hart would trust her again? She could only pray that day would come. Yet, she also had to ask herself if she honestly still trusted him.

"I have to look in on Gran too," she said.

The early-afternoon winter sun shone its frail but determined light into the windows, and as Jenny went upstairs she was even more aware of the dust on the banisters, the loose spots and stains on the stairs and the perpetual stale smell in the air.

She felt suddenly short of breath as she considered that she had to care for a failing grandmother, make the house more livable again, somehow find a job—which, she thought wholly discouraged now, would have *nothing* to do with her writing dream or any other dream for that matter—and, through all of this, keep things civil with the former love of her life who now seemed to remind her of every bad decision she'd ever made.

Her knees suddenly wobbled with the enormous weight of making impossible decisions. She felt her-self begin to go down...

And firm but gentle hands were supporting her and easing her into a sitting position.

Jenny drew rapid, shaky breaths, trying as her nerves frayed into pieces, to put other puzzle pieces together.

Of course, she knew it was David who supported her: his touch on her wiped out with lightning speed all the years she hadn't experienced it, and the spicy pine whiff of his aftershave swirled through her senses. But she inanely wondered how he had managed to be behind her when she thought he'd gone up ahead.

But what difference did it make? She was grateful he was there.

"Take slow, deep breaths," David was saying in a calming voice. "That's right. You'll be okay in just a minute." He no longer had his arm around her but, sitting on the steps, their arms and legs pressed warmly against each other.

As Jenny's breathing and heart rate slowed to a normal pace, she considered telling David that the ankle she'd twisted had given out on her again, causing the stumble, but he knew her far better than that. Not even Gran had ever seen what happened when something caused her take-charge attitude to crumble. It didn't happen often, but when self-doubt and fear of the future hit, it hit hard.

And only David had ever known how to get her through it.

So all she said now was "Thank you."

David was silent for a moment, breathing in unison with her, slipping again, she realized, into something he'd always done to ensure she was over the worst of it.

"It's a good thing I was there," he said quietly. "I would have already been upstairs except I thought I'd left my phone in the kitchen. Turns out it was in my pocket." He patted his pants.

"God's timing," Jenny said.

"Yes."

"So…what just happened here, Jen?"

Jenny knew there were more layers to that question than the physical aspect of her almost falling, and she thought about blaming the previously turned ankle, but she'd already made it clear that it wasn't bothering her anymore. Besides, this was David, and it didn't matter how many years they'd been apart: he would know she wasn't telling the truth.

So as they sat together on the stairs, she simply said, "I don't think I can do it."

"Do what?"

She threw her hands out in an expansively helpless gesture. "Anything—all of it."

"You can," David said after a beat of silence. "You will. One step at a time." His calm, level voice reminded her that he wasn't reassuring her because they were *David and Jenny* anymore and he believed in her, the way he believed the sun would rise every morning, but because it was his job to help people through their self-doubts and a myriad of other problems.

Still, she allowed herself to bask in the comfort for a minute or two.

Then David said so softly that she wasn't even sure that he meant her to hear, "You're not the only one who questions their ability to do what needs to be done."

"I don't imagine it's at all easy being a single parent," Jenny said. She resisted the urge to touch his arm, a gesture of comfort that she did not want to be misinterpreted.

David didn't say anything.

"Speaking of which," Jenny said, "you were on your way to check on them, and I still need to look in on Gran."

David nodded and stood up. He extended his hand to Jenny to help her up, and even though once again she knew it was merely politeness, not personal, the contact sent a familiar sensation racing through her, and she turned her head away so he wouldn't see her flush.

But, when she turned back, David was also looking away and didn't waste any time removing his hand.

Was he feeling something too?

Well, it didn't matter. She'd just admitted that she had more than enough on her plate. She didn't need old feelings dredged up to go along with everything else.

As Jenny was about to turn to go to Gran's room, David blurted out, "I just want you to know that you're not the only one who has tough decisions to make. Even when the repairs are done, I'm not sure if my house is ever going to feel like home anymore. I have to find a new location for my work, and as long as I'm venting here, I've been questioning whether the work I do has any real impact on anyone, and there are more days than not when I doubt that it does."

David breathed in and out in a visible effort to calm himself, while his eyes showed that he was already regretting his outburst.

This time Jenny didn't suppress her need to show she understood. She laid her hand on his arm.

"I think," she said, "that we both need to stop being a hindrance to each other."

David looked at her hand on his arm, then raised his eyes to hers.

"I agree," he said.

It wasn't exactly a resounding endorsement, but it was enough to still the whirlwind that had been raging through her.

At least for now.

It was Tuesday after supper, and Gran was in the parlor with the twins, showing them her enviable collection of music boxes. David could hear the delicate plinking of one playing the "Carousel Waltz," as he carried dishes from the table and handed them to Jenny to rinse.

In the days before Cheryl had made her unannounced departure, they had not been able to do the simplest of tasks together without a dark tension blooming between them.

He wasn't about to make comparisons, but it was easy to fall into a rhythm with Jenny, listening to her hum "Joy to the World" as he handed her the dishes.

She still had a lovely voice, he noted. No wonder she'd often been chosen as the female lead in the musicals at their high school and asked to sing solos in the church youth choir.

The sharing of grievances on Sunday had done them both good. They didn't make a lot of conversation, but when they did, they spoke easily of people they'd gone to school with, David updating Jenny on the ones she'd lost track of, and conversely, her having a surprising amount of news about others he no longer kept in touch with. As they chatted about high-school days, they managed to skate somewhat gracefully around the topic of how inseparable they had been.

When the kitchen was spotless, David found he felt no rush to end the camaraderie. He could still hear Estelle and the twins chatting and laughing, with music boxes accompanying them in the background.

An idea formed, and he acted on it before he could talk himself out of it.

"How'd you like to learn how to wield a hammer?"

Jenny narrowed her eyes at him but in a teasing way.

"Are you saying I don't know my way around a hammer, Hart?"

"What I'm saying, Powell, is that while you were

busy being a nightingale on stage, some of us grunts were breaking a sweat to give you the scenery to look good in."

They laughed together, then David dropped the joking tone.

"If you're going to live here, there are some things you should know about old houses. It would be way too expensive to call for a repair every time something went wrong."

It occurred to him as he spoke that for the first time he was letting himself believe that she did intend to stay and, maybe more importantly, he was letting Jenny know that he believed it.

Jenny nodded, her face somber, her eyes a bit panicked. It didn't take much to know that extra money wasn't something she currently had a whole lot of, if at all.

"I always did intend to help with the repairs," Jenny reminded him. "We just haven't been able to..." She faltered.

"We've been letting other stuff get in the way," David said, then corrected himself. "*I've* been letting other stuff get in the way. I'm going to do my best to stop that."

Jenny bit her lip thoughtfully. "Good," she said. "Because we get along too well not to get along...at least, we used to."

"Right," David said briskly, to counteract what the sight of her shining eyes did to him. "Okay, let's let Estelle and the girls know what we're up to."

After they had spoken to the others, with subtle but clear instructions that Rowe or Reba were to immediately come get them if something seemed amiss with Jenny's grandmother, David went to gather some basic tools and ushered Jenny over to some hinges that needed oiling.

As always when faced with a new task, Jenny Powell went at it with spirit and determination, and David remembered how much he had always enjoyed watching her take on a challenge.

For a little while, they worked side by side in a long-unused spare room, oiling hinges, securing loose pieces of carpet and dusting baseboards and window sills, all the while chatting with ease.

David occasionally offered a suggestion which Jenny accepted, and she was soon doing things at least as efficiently as he was.

"I was thinking…" he said.

"What?" Jenny stood up from her crouching position by one of the baseboards and stretched up on her tiptoes, extending her arms skyward and sighing with pleasure as the kink worked itself out of her back.

David was momentarily distracted.

Don't do that to yourself.

"I was thinking that once Christmas House is looking more like itself again, you could make some money from it—you know, charge admission for the daytime tours, and have a charge for the overnight guests."

This time, when Jenny narrowed her eyes at him there was no teasing in them. In fact, they had grown a bit frosty.

"No way," she said, shaking her head slowly back and forth for emphasis. "Not a chance. Gran would never forgive me if I started using Christmas House as a moneymaker. She and Gramps intended it to be a gift to the neighbors, something to bring some joy and solace in the midst of a hectic holiday season."

"Yeah, you're right," David conceded. For one thing, he was sick and tired of the animosity he'd been harboring against Jenny, and he just wanted those feelings to go away. But here he was slipping back into the habit of wanting to help her solve her problems.

He supposed that was an urge that was never going to go away, although it frightened him a little to think so.

Wanting to busy himself, he walked over to one of the windows and tested the latch to see how loose it was. A lightly flowery, soapy scent tickled his nose, and he realized that Jenny had followed him over.

"You are right about one thing," she said. "I definitely have to do something. What I was thinking is that I could write a story about bringing Christmas House back to life and bring in some of its history and what it's meant to people over the years."

"I think that sounds like something people would love to read about," David said.

The peacefulness that washed over him told him that it felt good to support Jenny's ideas again. It felt *right*.

"Dad?"

They both turned to see Reba in the doorway, tugging on a piece of her short hair, with a slightly anxious look in her eyes.

"Is everything okay?" Jenny asked, moving toward the door.

"I think so," Reba said hesitantly. "I mean, your gran isn't hurt or anything. I asked Rowe to stay with her."

"That was a smart thing to do," Jenny praised her. "But I can tell something is worrying you. I'll come with you."

She put her hands on Reba's shoulders and gently

turned her to head back downstairs. With a look over her shoulder, she signaled that David should follow.

"She started asking about someone named Bess," Reba explained as they went downstairs. "She wondered where she was, and it looked like she was getting a little upset, like she might cry or something. We didn't know who Bess was," she added apologetically.

"That's okay," Jenny said encouragingly. "There's no reason why you should know that. Bess is my mother," she explained. "She and my dad are in Peru right now helping people learn about Jesus."

They reached the bottom of the stairs, and Reba paused and turned, her small face still troubled.

"Didn't she tell your Gran where she was going?"

With a quick glance in David's direction, Jenny said, "She did tell her. But Gran is just a bit forgetful sometimes. It's just something that can happen to people when they get older. It's really nice that you are concerned about her, Reba. That shows you're a caring person."

Reba smiled shyly.

"I'll talk to Gran and remind her where my mom is," Jenny said. "Thank you very much for telling us."

"Would you mind sending Rowena my way?" David asked. "And, by the way, thank you."

"Why are you thanking me?" Jenny asked.

"For being honest with Reba," David said. "And for always being kind and patient with my girls. That means a lot to me."

He knew it couldn't be easy for Jenny to give Reba a calm, simple explanation for her grandmother's behavior—not when signs of the elderly woman's decline were so troubling to her.

Jenny furrowed her brow in puzzlement. "I can't imagine that anyone would want to be anything other than kind and patient with your girls. They are both sweethearts."

"Thank you," David said. He shook his head, troubled by his own neglect. "I realized I haven't even asked about your cancer, if it ever resurfaced, except I'm sure I would have heard, at least something, if it had. I didn't mean to… It's just that—"

"It's okay," Jenny said in a hurry to reassure him. "It's stayed in remission, so I've been very blessed that way."

The silence that fell between them made David wonder if they were both wondering the same thing: If Reba's or Jenny's cancer resurfaced, would they still trust in the Lord's blessings?

It was a question he fervently hoped he wouldn't have to answer.

But what presently troubled him was how strongly and undeniably he still cared about how Jenny was doing.

Rowena came out as requested. "Can we explore the house more?" she asked.

"Let's see how Jenny's grandmother is doing first," David suggested. Then realizing that Rowe would also want to know, he explained who Bess was and that she was away for a while.

"Okay." Rowena scuffed her toe in the carpet and was uncharacteristically quiet, while Reba wandered into the living room across from the parlor, sat down on a bench and softly touched the keys of an old organ. Then she touched them with more deliberateness and pumped the pedals with her feet. A wheezing chord sounded, which made her jump and giggle.

David waited for Rowe to laugh too or at least to boss Reba to be quiet. But she remained quiet.

"Is everything okay, Rowe?" he asked. "I know it must have been troubling to see Mrs. Winters getting upset, but Jenny is with her now. She'll be okay."

"I know." Rowena heaved a shuddering sigh that echoed through David as he realized that she was trying not to cry.

Ah, his tough little Rowe. His heart ached with regret. She so convincingly played the role of having a thick skin that he willingly let himself be talked into believing it. Probably, he acknowledged with shame, because if he could convince himself that Rowena was strong, it gave him one less thing to worry about.

He silently made a promise to God that, with His help, he would do better. He loved both of his girls with everything he had to give and never, ever wanted their concerns to be a burden.

"Rowe," he said gently, "what is it, sweetheart?"

She didn't answer but continued her toe scuffing.

"Rowe, whatever you're feeling, you know you can tell me. Everything you think and feel is important to me, and I'm very sorry if I don't always let you know that."

Rowena raised her head.

"I just… I just was thinking about Jenny's mom being gone. She must miss her."

Then she hardened her face in a way that devastated David, because a little girl should never have to be that tough.

"I guess…even if she misses her, she'll be okay. Me and Reba are."

David gathered his daughter into his arms.

"It's okay not to be okay," he told her. Those were words he'd spoken many times to his clients and had long ago promised himself that they would never be just words. He always wanted to offer them a safe space to sort out what was okay in their lives and what needed work. If he did that for people he was only professionally acquainted with, there was no doubt that he owed at least that much to his daughters.

Because clearly Rowena wasn't okay with what had happened, no matter how strong a front she tried to put up.

Their holiday time together was passing quickly, and he had been frittering it away with his own worries and his irritation over Jenny Powell reappearing in his life.

Well, there would be no more of that.

Dear Lord, I make a lot of mistakes, but not being there for the beautiful daughters You blessed me with would be the worst one of all. Please help me to be a better parent. Please help us find joy in this season of the birth Your son.

Jenny came out of the parlor looking subdued but calm. At David's questioning look, she said, "Gran is fine. She's got things straight in her head, for now."

The *for now* echoed in David's head, and he swallowed, sympathetic about the long road he already knew Jenny could have ahead of her.

But now was the time to focus on his daughters.

Reba was now laboriously plunking out "Away in a Manger" on the asthmatic organ, and he caught her eye and beckoned to her to come out and join them.

"Rowe asked if you could explore the attic again," David said.

"I can go up there with them," Jenny offered. "Thanks again, by the way, for fixing the stairs."

"You're welcome," David said. He tried to shrug it off like it was nothing, but he couldn't help the surge of pleasure that went through him knowing he had done something to help her and seeing the light of gratitude on her face.

Jenny had always helped him in more ways than he could explain or count. She always made sure that he knew he mattered, that he had gifts to share. Of course, she did that for everyone: it was one of *her* great gifts. Anytime he had the opportunity to give back to her, he had always been willing to do so.

Apparently, he still was.

He realized that the others were still waiting for his answer.

"You could go up and explore the attic," he said. "Or—" he paused dramatically "—now that it's snowed more, we could go out and have a sleigh ride around town and look at all the lights and the decorations and end up at Murphy's for some hot cocoa. How does that sound?"

Reba called out, "Yes! Yes! Yes!" while Rowe nodded, broadly smiling after a fleeting effort at being nonchalant.

"That's a great idea," Jenny said. "You'll have a wonderful time."

Was David imagining it, or did her smile look a bit sad?

"Aren't you coming with us?" Reba asked, voicing the question he wasn't sure he should ask.

He glanced at Rowena, remembering her reference to her mother's absence earlier. He didn't want to do anything to upset her.

But Rowena still basked in the excitement of going out after dark to do something different and fun.

And, foolish or not, he really, *really* wanted Jenny to come with them.

He turned to her, "Please join us," he said. "I would really like that."

Chapter Eleven

Things happened in a whirlwind, but Jenny couldn't deny that she was happy that they had.

Gran had gone early to bed, which made her hesitant to go out, but at David's suggestion, she called a neighbor, who was willing to bring her evening reading and knitting over to the house so that someone would be there just in case Gran needed anything.

"Well, Jenny Powell, as I live and breathe!" the sleigh driver, Joe McFayden, greeted her. "It's so nice to have you home for Christmas." Like everyone else—except David—he was tactful and didn't mention all the Christmases that she *hadn't* come home.

Meanwhile, Rowe and Reba patted the soft noses of the horses with their mittened hands. Puffs of frosty air made clouds around the horses' large nostrils.

Soon Jenny found herself bundled into a sleigh—she sat beside Reba and David sat across from her with Rowe—and when the driver of the sleigh covered their legs with a warm blue blanket, tucking it in securely, it brought back a rush of memories.

For all she knew, it could be the exact same blanket.

Joe McFayden was the same as he'd always been, his hair a bit whiter and thinner, and his back slightly stooped, but still with that smile that said there was hope and promise in the world and that he wanted to help people discover that.

In his real job, he had been the principal at Living Skies Elementary School for many years before his retirement, doing his best to instill that same way of thinking in the teachers and students that came through the doors.

Joe looked between her and David with a kindly, questioning expression but chose not to say anything. But there was no doubt, Jenny thought, that he must be wondering what she was doing back and why she was with David and his daughters.

More memories flooded in.

She and David had taken countless sleigh rides together, from the year when they jostled and shoved at one another and loudly wished that the horses would go faster, to the years when they sat together snuggled close, sharing the blue blanket and thinking about what their Christmases together in the future might look like.

The slightly sorrowful smile and faraway look in David's eyes made her wonder if he was having the same kind of memories.

But no, he had made many memories without her, and there was no reason to think he was being nostalgic about any time they'd spent together.

That realization made Jenny's heart ache, and a coldness come over her that wasn't caused by the frosty air that surrounded them.

Then Reba tugged at her arm in a burst of excitement

as the horses began their easy trot, leaving the park and heading toward the center of the town.

Joe pulled out his iPhone and turned on some music. He used to use a radio, Jenny recalled, so it seemed he had upgraded. Soon, the opening refrains of "Jingle Bells" rang out, and Jenny gave Reba's hand an answering squeeze as excitement swept through her too.

Then she saw David noticing their little exchange and couldn't read the expression on his face, which made her slightly nervous.

Soon, though, they were all absorbed in pointing and exclaiming over the displays of lights and lawn ornaments. Living Skies really did like to go all out at Christmas.

As they passed a front yard that resembled a snowman family reunion, Jenny's heart tugged with regret that Gran wasn't with them. She always loved seeing the lights and maybe seeing them now would encourage her to put some effort into her own house.

But, Jenny reminded herself, Gran wasn't ignoring what needed to be done out of laziness. She was older, clearly tired more easily and...simply not completely Gran anymore.

David caught her eye as the twins were pointing and laughing at a snowman wearing a Santa Claus beard and hat.

"What's wrong?" he mouthed at her.

She smiled and shook her head.

But he said, "Rowe, trade places with me. Jenny and I need to talk for a minute."

The young girl's look fell on Jenny like an icicle.

"It's fine," Jenny said hurriedly. "It can wait. I was

just thinking about Gran and the house," she explained, looking at David.

"Okay." He looked like he was about to say more but didn't.

Rowena snuggled into her father's side and pointed at a house.

"Mom always said these were her favorite colors, remember?" she said, indicating a yard where the house and the pine trees in the yard were strung with baubles and tinsel in blue, gold and silver.

"I do remember," David said quietly, and Jenny sensed that he was restraining himself from checking her reaction.

But she knew it was one of those situations where it was better to stay quiet.

Beside her, Reba was also quiet, with a pensive expression.

Then David said, "Can we go by the church now, Joe?" and Rowe and Reba both sat forward and clapped their hands.

On Sunday, after the service, they had seen a group of volunteers carting out big boxes and large cardboard shapes, which signaled that the Nativity display was going up.

"Yes, the church," Rowena agreed happily, "and then hot chocolate."

So the evening wasn't going to come to an end quite yet.

Dear Lord, Jenny prayed silently, *whatever my feelings are toward David, and You know I'm still trying to sort that out, please help me to be a friend and helper to his daughters who miss their mother. I pray that You heal their hearts and help them to know that You will never leave them.*

Of course, she was in no position to judge someone for leaving.

When the sleigh stopped in front of the church, Jenny's thoughts grew still as she was both awed and comforted by the reminder of Who they celebrated.

The large, outdoor Nativity display at Good Shepherd Church was truly a work of art that drew people into a time of reflection and gratitude.

The serene expression on Mary's face as she bent over her newborn son caused a nameless ache in Jenny's heart. She handed that ache over to God knowing He would understand.

The Nativity seemed to have soothed them all because by the time they were dropped off at Murphy's, both of the girls were including their father and Jenny in their chatter as if the moment of melancholy on the ride had never happened.

Jenny watched Joe wave away David's attempts to tip him and smiled, thinking that there was something else that hadn't changed.

Murphy's was busy for a Tuesday night, which was understandable as it was the holiday season. Somehow Jenny had let herself forget that a busy place meant many curious sets of eyes.

She put on a bright smile and waved a general hello to the room, but she was glad when they were ushered to a table in the overflow room at the back. It meant that they would have to walk past all of the tables to get there but would have some semblance of privacy once they were settled.

Not that they needed privacy.

Even though the hot chocolate was as sweet and delicious as she remembered, and she willingly pretended, along with David, that they didn't know they had whipped cream on their noses, because it was so delightful to hear the twins laughing, the unnamable sense of loss, sprinkled with the lightest dash of apprehension lingered, and Jenny hid her relief behind another bright smile when their bill arrived to signal that the evening was almost over.

I'm just worried about Gran, she told herself. But as she watched David helping Reba put her coat on, she knew that there was a great web of emotions in her heart that needed to be untangled.

When Jenny woke up the next day, she was determined to stop lingering in regrets of the past or apprehension about the future. So instead of letting herself snooze for a few more minutes, she sprung up and hurried to the bathroom to freshen up, then pulled on her most comfortable pair of blue jeans and a sweater in the teal-blue color that David had told her brought out her eyes.

Not that she was wearing it for David, and she certainly wasn't thinking of him when she dabbed on a shiny lip gloss, nor when she pinned her hair behind her ears was she thinking about how he had told her that when she wore her hair that way it highlighted her cheekbones.

No, her goal for the day wasn't to impress someone but to pitch her new story idea to Natalie and pray that she'd get the go-ahead. She'd had a hard time falling asleep the night before and had slept fitfully when she did. So as the earliest reasonable time to get out of bed had rolled around, Jenny had been a mixture of weariness and determination.

There was no way she was wasting another day dwelling on the what-ifs. She was going to kick-start her writing career, and she was going to continue to bring improvements to Gran's home—*her* home—learning as much as she could along the way, until she was wholly confident in her own abilities.

Because as much as she cared about David, she didn't want to need him, especially knowing that he had his own things to deal with.

When Jenny went into the kitchen for breakfast, she was sharply reminded of the latter.

David clutched his cell phone against his ear while he rubbed his chin with the other hand. His mouth was drawn in a tight line, and his bleary eyes gave every indication that he'd had an even worse night than hers.

He hung the phone up and placed it facedown on the table.

Seeing that the twins were preoccupied spooning jam onto their toast and that Gran had a faraway smile on her face as she held her teacup and gazed out the kitchen window, Jenny took the opportunity to catch David's eye and ask in an undertone, "What's wrong?"

"How much time do you have?" For once, there were no barriers in his brown eyes.

Jenny answered, "I have all the time you need."

"Well, two things are going on, and they impact each other." He paused and spread butter on his toast, then picked it up and looked at it like he couldn't remember why he'd thought he might want to eat it.

"You know I've been getting a lot of pressure to give

up the office space I've been renting," David said, putting the toast down on his plate.

She nodded, encouraging David to continue.

"That was Leo on the phone," David said. "I asked him to give me until after the New Year to find new office space, and he'd backed off for a few days, so I thought I was in the clear." The weariness in his eyes visibly deepened. "But apparently not."

Jenny grimaced. "So he's putting the pressure on again?"

"You could say that, yeah." David tugged at his earlobe, a habit when his stress levels were high. "I mean, I do get that he's anxious for a new start in his own life, and he's afraid of losing the opportunity to sell the property if he doesn't act fast, but still…"

Outside the window, big flakes of snow began to fall. Gran clapped her hands together like a child and beckoned Rowe and Reba to follow her to the window to watch winter's beautiful, icy dance.

"You said a couple of things are going on," Jenny prodded gently, "and that one impacts the other?"

"The other part of it has to do with my work," David said. "And it's confidential."

"Okay, I understand."

"Let's just say people need me, and I need a place where I can help them."

He picked up his toast then and took a bite from it, chewing as if he wished he could make his problems disappear in a similar fashion.

"But the worst thing of all," he said, after swallowing, "is that this is supposed to be a time for the girls and me. I'm supposed to meet Leo this afternoon, as a matter of fact, and I don't know what they're going to do."

"They can hang out with me," Jenny said firmly. "I just need some time this morning to take care of something, and then I'm all yours."

The words hung between them on a bittersweet thread. No, she would never be all his again, nor would he be hers, but that didn't mean that she didn't care enough to help a friend.

She cared, all right… Maybe she cared too much.

David didn't know if he should be relieved or hurt that his daughters were nonchalant about him being unable to spend time with them that afternoon. It was no comfort to remind himself that they'd been through worse.

Jenny came home with the news that Natalie had agreed to look at her revised idea for a story, and even though she had received no promises that it would go to print, there was a determination on her face that David instantly recognized.

Dear Lord, help me to be an encouragement in Jenny's life, not a hindrance—and in the lives of others too, he added hastily.

"You must be anxious to get started." He looked from her to the girls, who were again watchful, waiting to see what would happen next.

"Nope, I've got it all up here for later." Jenny tapped her head with one finger, a pseudo-wise expression on her face. David knew she was clowning, to put him and especially the girls at ease.

It was a classic Jenny Powell move, and one that made him smile, despite the tangle of circumstances he was trying to unravel.

"So what are we going to do this afternoon?" she asked the girls.

David could tell by the way their eyes met and the head tilt that Rowena gave Reba, encouraging her to speak up, that they had discussed something between themselves.

"We need Christmas dresses," Reba said. Her soft voice wavered slightly, and her eyes nervously scanned her father's face for a reaction.

Why would she think he'd be upset about that?

Now that Reba had opened the door, Rowe stepped in. She folded her arms and lifted her chin.

"Mom always got us new dresses for Christmas," she declared. "We want new dresses."

"Except we don't want them matching," Reba added, more confident with her sister's support. "Because we're too old for that now."

David took in his daughters' faces: Reba's anxious and hopeful, Rowena's defiant, which he understood was its own breed of anxiousness. The problem was that he didn't know if they wanted to go shopping with Jenny because they truly wanted the dresses and thought it would be a fun experience, or if it was something they had cooked up between them to make the point again that they missed their mother and Jenny wasn't her.

He mentally shook the thought away. Stress was doing a number on him. *Dear Lord, forgive me for doubting my own daughters.*

"I'd love to take you shopping," Jenny declared with enthusiasm. "I'm sure Debra will have some beautiful dresses in."

David suddenly remembered a soft, sky-blue dress with a skirt that twirled that Jenny had worn to a dance they attended together and he swallowed, remembering a time when life had seemed to stretch out before them with endless possibilities and cancer—or Jenny leaving him—wasn't even the barest whisper of a fear.

But now they were friends, or something in the cautious friendish category, and he was grateful for that. If he'd been asked a couple of months ago if he thought his daughters would ever go shopping with Jenny Powell, he wouldn't have known whether to laugh or cry at a question that was beyond absurd.

But God did work in mysterious ways. He could almost hear Estelle's voice saying it.

"But your Gran…" as the realization struck him.

"She'll probably want to come with us," Jenny said in an unruffled way. "And if she doesn't, I'm sure I can ask a neighbor to look in."

David knew how worried Jenny was about her grandmother, so the effort she was making to assure his girls that their request wasn't any trouble touched him.

Estelle, in fine form, waved away the fuss about what she was going to do. "I'll stay here and read a book or watch some television," she said. "I'm perfectly capable of keeping myself entertained."

"I'll call one of the neighbors, anyway," Jenny murmured to David. "They can pretend they popped by to borrow a cup of sugar."

"Do people still *do* that?"

They laughed, and their eyes met.

"Thank you," David said. "You have no idea how much this helps me…us."

He squeezed her hands, and suddenly it was like he was that teenage boy again telling his best friend that he liked her as much more than a friend. It was all he could do not to lean in to kiss her, especially when her blue eyes shone with something shy and hopeful, something so akin to that night that he thought she must be remembering it too.

Rowena coughed loudly, and the bubble that encased them popped and disappeared.

David groaned inwardly and hoped that he hadn't ruined the shopping trip. He wanted his daughters to like Jenny, because he liked having her back in his life.

Not that she was *back*. But she wasn't gone either, not anymore.

"Come on, girls," Jenny said breezily, as if that moment hadn't passed between them. "Let's put on some good shopping clothes."

"What are good shopping clothes?" David asked.

Rowena and Reba also raised questioning faces.

"Anything that doesn't have a lot of buttons," Jenny declared. "If you have a lot of trying on to do, you don't want buttons to slow things down."

"Ah, the mysteries of women shopping," David smiled and shook his head.

But his heart swelled with love for his daughters and gratitude to Jenny for helping them.

Sometime later, David was in his car headed to a neighboring small town. Yorkville was only about a thirty minute drive from Living Skies, but somehow it had always felt more distant than that to him. The drive went quickly, but when he was there, the difference in the small towns was apparent, with Living Skies giving off a much more energetic and hopeful vibe.

He had been asked to make a call on a young single mother, who was struggling to parent a four-year-old boy. They weren't his usual kind of client, and he rarely made house calls. But, their usual caseworker had been called away on a family emergency, and as David drove, his skin prickled with a nervous but energizing apprehension that he hadn't felt for a long time.

It wasn't that he didn't respect his current clientele or want the best for them. But their problems were usually about wanting their children to get into good universities and not being able to get them to do the work, or to excel at sports or at playing a musical instrument or whatever it took to stand out from the crowd.

Occasionally, there would be a fear that a child was abusing drugs or alcohol, and he would counsel the parents on open communication, provide signs to watch for and recommend programs.

David would never dismiss anyone's problems or concerns as unimportant, but as he approached Yorkville's town sign and eased up on the gas pedal, he realized that it had been a long time since he had felt like the work he did made a real difference in someone's life.

The Lord knew that he was struggling to make a difference in his own daughters' lives.

He and Jenny had always been so sure that together they were going to make a difference. Well, they weren't together, but maybe he could do his own part.

And, Lord, he prayed, *help Jenny to know that she still has so much to offer too. I want her to have a happy and fulfilling life.*

His heart gave an odd twist as he realized how much he really did want that for her.

He would just have to make himself stop wanting to still be part of it.

But now it was time to focus on the task at hand. David pulled up to a small house where peeling paint and a pile of snow in front of a garage were just two of the signs that the occupant was too overwhelmed with meeting daily obligations to have time to do anything about them.

He walked cautiously up the icy steps, clinging to the railing and making a mental note to attend to them, even if it was on his own time.

He knocked on the door, and after waiting a minute, rang the doorbell.

The door opened slowly, and he was faced with a pale woman with lank ash-blond hair and a sharp-featured face that mingled fear and defiance. She was even younger than David had expected, and he battled a surge of unprofessional emotions.

The little boy that clung to her hand had a runny nose and the same color hair, although his had some curl in it. His eyes, also the same hazel as his mother's, were wide and questioning.

"What do you want?" the young woman asked.

"Are you Tiffany Bower?" David asked.

"Who wants to know?"

The little boy wiped his nose with the back of the hand that wasn't clutching his mother's.

Two sets of eyes were wary and watchful.

"My name is David Hart," David explained. "Roberta Ferris was called away on an emergency, and she asked me to drop in on you and see how things were going."

Tiffany paused for a long moment, then opened the door, as if pushing an unbearable weight, to allow him to come in.

About forty-five minutes later, David drove off with the uneasy certainty that he was going to have to recommend that the little boy be placed into foster care. He didn't doubt that his mother was doing the best that she could but he had seen the struggle she was having to provide adequate care.

As he inched his car along the ruts of the unplowed street, he realized he desperately wanted to talk to Jenny about it. He couldn't, of course—his work was confidential—but she had always been the one who could chase away those times when he lost his belief that there was a light in a dark situation.

He wondered how her shopping trip with the girls was going. He let his mind wander to them chatting and laughing, squeals of excitement as they found the perfect dresses. It was a far more pleasant visual than the nearly empty fridge and black mold edging the windowsills of the home he had just left.

Just as he was about to leave the town limits, David saw it: a small, brick building with the sign Office Space for Rent.

But I can't move my office out here...can I?

Chapter Twelve

Debra's was the same as Jenny remembered: full of huge racks of dresses and an even bigger aura of hope and excitement.

The walls were still painted a glossy peach color and the proprietor, Debra Miller, still had a knack for artfully displaying the merchandise.

You will look at dresses, Jenny told herself. *You will help the girls pick out dresses and maybe find one for yourself. You will* not *think about how you think David Hart maybe, just maybe, wanted to kiss you.*

She also would not think about how ready she had been to kiss him back.

Thankfully, further distraction from the troubling thought came in the form of Debra herself exiting a back room and rushing toward Jenny, her arms wide open for a hug.

The small, slightly plump and always energetic Indigenous woman's hair had more gray in it than it used to, and the laugh lines that creased her round face were more prominent, but as Jenny welcomed her into her embrace, breathing in the scent of fresh lemon, she knew that Debra was the same in all the ways that mattered.

"You're too thin," Debra commented as she stepped back, her eyes kind but appraising. "I saw you at church, actually. I'm sorry I didn't get a chance to say hello."

Her gaze flickered to the twins, but if she thought it was odd that they were here with Jenny, her smile didn't show it.

"Hi, girls," she greeted them. A tapered finger sagely tapped the side of her nose. "It must be time for Christmas dresses, am I right?"

Their smiles broke out like bright lights on trees.

Soon they were off to the dressing room with an armful of dresses each.

"We can help each other button," Reba assured Jenny.

Jenny browsed a rack of adult party dresses. Even while she asked herself what she could possibly need one for, it was still hard to resist the lure of sparkling gold and silver, or the satiny sheen and velvet caress of reds and greens.

She couldn't resist picking up one that was like a dark blue sky dotted with silver stars and holding it up against her.

"That would look perfect on you." Debra tilted her head in an appraising manner. "Any special occasions coming up?"

Although Jenny had always trusted Debra, there was a curiosity in that question that she wasn't prepared to address yet…even if she'd known how to answer it.

She was saved from having to do so when the girls came out of the dressing room and stood in front of her, both awkward and hopeful.

They had both chosen dresses in shades of green, and

while Rowe was striking in her jade dress with gold fili-
gree trim on the princess neckline and at the end of the
long fitted sleeves and showed signs of the beauty she
was growing into, Reba's emerald choice washed her
out. Her pale skin and shadowed eyes made Jenny ache.

But they were all in this together. Even though she
wasn't sure at all if they even wanted her input.

Rowena sought out a mirror that clearly told her what
she wanted to know based on the way she lifted her
head and took up the full skirt in her hands, swishing
it back and forth.

Reba found a mirror too, and when Jenny saw Reba's
thin arms dangling at her sides, while her face collapsed
into disappointment, she prayed for the right words.

"That's not quite right, is it?" It was best to be honest, Jenny decided. Reba was a smart girl, and she'd
be doing her no favors with false flattery. The shop
was full of dresses. They could surely find something
more suitable.

Reba quickly averted her eyes from her reflection and
shook her head.

"Would you like me to help you find something?"
Jenny offered.

"Rowe, why don't you come up front with me?"
Debra asked, reading the situation accurately, for which
Jenny was grateful. "I can show you some matching
hairbands and ribbons."

Rowena went happily off with Debra to look at ac-
cessories, and Reba drew in a shuddering breath, then
clamped her lips tight and nodded.

"Yes, please."

She slipped her hand into Jenny's, and tears that

Jenny had held back at seeing the girl's disappointment with her appearance slipped out at this gesture of trust.

She turned away briefly, murmuring an excuse about something in her eye, then turned back, her smile determined. Raising Reba's hand in a gesture of victory she said, "Let's do this!"

A little while later, a cherry-red velvet dress with snowflake buttons down the front and white faux-fur cuffs on the long sleeves was pronounced the winner. It brought a flush of color into Reba's cheeks and caused her eyes to light up in a way that made her whole face beautiful.

Rowe showed Reba and Jenny a sparkling gold headband she had chosen, and after they helped Reba pick out a barrette that resembled holly in snow, they were ready to check out.

Jenny stopped her eyes from drifting again to the blue and silver dress, telling herself again that she had no use for it even if she could afford it.

"I'd love to help you find something too, Jenny," Debra offered.

"That's okay," Jenny assured her.

The girls beamed and, for once, Reba's hand didn't gravitate up to check her hair's growth.

"David said…" Jenny stopped. Using his name just felt too personal when she knew Debra was reining in her curiosity like a bridled horse.

"Their dad said to bill the purchases to his account."

"Of course," Debra jotted a quick note, then leaned forward, as if eager for a good catch-up session.

The shop door opened, and Natalie Surasik entered. "Hey, Jenny," she greeted her. "What brings you here?" Then her eyes swept over the twins, holding the bags with their new dresses.

"Jenny took us shopping," Rowe answered. "For new Christmas dresses."

"I can see that," Natalie said. "How nice."

Maybe it was because she knew that Natalie was an editor with an unrelenting urge to get the story, but the glint in her eyes made Jenny nervous.

"How are you *feeling*, sweetheart?" Natalie asked Reba, who shrugged, obviously uncomfortable.

"She's doing great!" Jenny answered. "And we have to get going."

She put one hand on each of the girls' shoulders and steered them toward the door, thanking Debra again as she did so.

She respected Natalie and wanted to work for the paper, yes. But that didn't mean she appreciated her fawning over Reba in that probing way.

"Jenny, about your story…" Natalie said, causing Jenny to pause at the door and turn back. Apprehension crept up her neck on tiny spider legs.

But Natalie was smiling. "I've thought more about your story, about Christmas House, and I like it. Go ahead and write it."

"Really?" Jenny asked, wishing she could be more excited. "But what happens if you don't like it?"

Natalie waved the concern away. "It's not a big deal if I have to polish it up. That's what editors do."

"Okay…well, thank you."

Walking along with a twin on each side, Jenny's troubled thoughts weaved around their happy chatter.

Why can't I be happy about this, Lord? Have I been

worried about things for so long that I don't recognize good news when I get it?

Then she remembered two things: they had to pass by the newspaper office to get to Debra's…and she couldn't recollect ever seeing Natalie wear a dress for any occasion.

But when they arrived back at the house, they were greeted by a screaming smoke detector and a grim-faced David on the front steps, which chased all other thoughts from Jenny's mind.

"What's going on?" she gasped. "Gran…?" She couldn't find the words as panic rippled through her.

"She's okay," David said. "But it's a good thing I got back when I did."

It turned out that Gran was inside the door, just behind David. She peered around him, with a slightly disgruntled expression.

"I just wanted to bake more cookies," she said.

What bothered Jenny the most was that, although Gran was clearly irritated that her cookies had burned, she did not seem to be fully cognizant of the seriousness of the situation.

Her heart sunk like a stone, and the girls, who had been so excited to show off their new dresses, were frozen, wide-eyed.

"It's okay." As David bent over and swept them both into his arms, above their heads his eyes locked with Jenny's. She could still read those eyes as well as she could read her own in a mirror, and she saw only understanding in them.

Later, after the girls had modeled their dresses to high praise and they'd all had supper and played a game of checkers, Jenny took Gran up to her room and helped her into bed.

She sat at her bedside holding her hands, looking into her beloved face and praying that God would reveal to her what she had to do.

I think I know, dear Lord. I just don't know if I have the strength to do it.

"You're mad at me," Gran said.

"No, I'm not." Jenny squeezed her hands. "But you did put a scare into all of us," she added. "And, to be honest, Gran, it worries me, you being in the house alone if things like this are going to happen. I can't be here all the time."

Gran's face crumpled, reminding Jenny of Reba's face in the shop, before they'd managed to find the perfect dress for her.

"It's okay," Jenny hurried to reassure her grandmother, despite her continued misgivings. "No harm, no foul," she quoted her late grandfather, trying to make her smile.

Gran gave out the consolation prize of a watery half smile.

"We'll figure it all out," Jenny said, as much to herself as to Gran and also sending it up as a prayer.

This appeared to calm Gran. She squeezed Jenny's hands, then tugged the covers up to her chin with a sigh.

"Talk to David," she said, as her eyes drifted closed. "He'll help you figure it out. That's what couples do."

Jenny continued to sit. She told herself that it was to ensure her grandmother settled into a deep sleep. But she knew it was to try to assuage her wounded heart before facing the smoky smell downstairs again and what it could mean for Gran's future.

Jenny didn't know what hurt her more, the confusion that made Gran believe that she and David were still a couple or realizing how much she wished that were true.

David praised the girls' dress choices once more, then asked them to go up to their room and get changed and to stay up there while things got sorted downstairs.

"It does smell smoky," Rowena wrinkled her nose and Reba nodded, so they were both happy to oblige his request.

Having little choice to clear the smoke, David had cracked open the kitchen window. Thankfully, it was a mild evening for mid-December in Saskatchewan.

He had discarded the burned cookies, and as he took a cloth and wiped around the counters and stove, he thought and prayed.

Had God been giving him a sign by sending him out on a call that he wouldn't normally go on, thereby allowing him to see that space for rent?

He didn't know.

What he did know was that, no matter how much he talked about helping Jenny fix up this house and giving his daughters a good Christmas, nothing was happening the way he planned.

Maybe the only signs he should be paying attention to were the ones that told him to hurry Leo up on the renovations, find a place for his office and face the truth that maybe Christmas would never be what it used to be.

Jenny came into the kitchen, and his heart was torn between being attracted to how she looked in her slim-fitting jeans and loose-knit periwinkle sweater and an ache for the troubled expression on her face.

"Would you like some tea?" he offered.

She shook her head, sitting down in one of the kitchen chairs. "No...but can we talk?"

He must have looked wary because she hurried to assure him, "I just need a friend."

"I can be that," David said quietly and joined her at the table.

"It's still a little smoky in here and a bit chilly." Jenny hugged herself, shivering a little.

"I'm sorry," David said. "I had to open a window. I should close it now. I don't want any pipes to burst. Believe me, you don't ever want *that* to happen."

It was strange, though, even as he said it, the problems in his own home seemed faraway and a bit unreal.

Maybe that had something to do with sitting in Estelle's kitchen with a blue-eyed woman, whose gaze had the power to make him forget all the lost years between them.

"We could go sit in the parlor," Jenny offered.

"Sounds good." He wondered if she too was remembering all of the hours they'd spent there, chatting about everything, sorting out life's questions.

It had all seemed so easy then.

Times had definitely changed, but the way Jenny plopped herself into the cushy yellow-gold armchair, sinking into its worn cushion, immediately took David back all those years.

Instinctively, he sat in the matching chair, legs stretched out in front of him.

They both had things they needed to talk about, he knew, but he needed just a moment to enjoy the feeling of being suspended in another time before cancer, broken relationships and real-estate problems.

"Do you still read the classics?" he asked.

If the question caught Jenny off guard, she didn't show it.

"I still try to reread Ivanhoe once a year."

"No kidding?" David felt a grin split his face. "Me too."

Hearing that he and Jenny shared that habit somehow pleased him very much.

"Do your girls like to read?" Jenny asked. Apparently, she too was willing to stall the conversation about more worrisome matters, at least for the time being.

"Rowena is into graphic novels," David said. "I figure, why not? At least she's reading something, right?"

"Of course," Jenny agreed. "Besides, if you listen to book blogs, they're definitely getting more acceptance and respect as their own genre. What about Reba? Does she read them too?

"No." David shook his head. "She's our classics girl."

His tongue stumbled as he heard himself say *our*, but Jenny nodded, encouraging him to continue.

"She's already read *Little Women*," David said. "I'm not sure she understood all of it, and we had to have a long talk about Beth's death, especially…well, you know."

This time Jenny didn't even have to nod. Her eyes said it all. She did know.

"But she loves to read," David finished. "And she's not afraid to ask questions."

"They're lovely girls," Jenny said. "Both of them."

"They are," David agreed. "I won't pretend I'm not biased, but hearing you say it helps me trust that I'm not completely off track."

"You're definitely not."

"I keep promising them a great Christmas." He sat up

and drew in his legs, moving his hands from the back of his head and flexing his fingers opened and closed on his thighs. "But I haven't kept my promise."

By saying the words, he ended their short reprieve of pretending that they had nothing more to worry about than what books to read next.

"You said you wanted to talk," he prompted Jenny. He would rather listen and see if he could be of some help than try to untangle his own issues.

Jenny sat up straighter, confirming that the brief interlude for idle chitchat was over.

"Just a sec," Jenny said. She got up and switched on the standing lamp with a pale green shade that darker green tassels dangled from.

She returned to her chair and said, "First of all, thank you again. If you hadn't come back when you did …" She shuddered.

"You don't have to thank me," David said. "A lot of people would say that was just pure dumb luck and good timing, though I prefer to think God had a hand in that timing."

"I think so too, but it doesn't change the hard facts, does it?"

"The hard facts meaning…" David told himself not to suspect that she was just preparing her reason for leaving again.

"Gran needs round-the-clock care," Jenny said. "I plan on staying," she mused, answering the unspoken question that kept tormenting him. "But, I will be working, I mean, I *have* to work, eventually, whether it's writing or whatever I can find, and I can't be with her every second. So I've come to realize that—" her teeth gnawed her lower lip "—and that's probably the hardest part, but then there's what comes next. If Gran stays here, who's going to help me look after her? If she has to live somewhere else, where's it going to be? How will I afford it?"

She got up and began to pace, lines of tension bracketing her mouth.

David watched her anxiously, monitoring for signs of another anxiety attack.

He wished he could give her answers. More than anything, almost more than he wanted answers for himself. He caught his breath when he realized how much he also wanted to take her in his arms to console her, to kiss the top of her sugar- and apple-scented hair.

But he wouldn't—couldn't—do that. Instead he suggested, "We could pray together."

Jenny hesitated slightly, then sat down and extended her hands to his. As soon as their hands clasped together, David knew that he had made the wrong call. Not that it was ever the wrong time for two believers to pray together, but he hadn't anticipated that doing so would feel much more intimate and powerful than a simple hug from a friend might have.

While he struggled to find his voice, Jenny began, not only asking that the Lord help her make the best decisions regarding Gran but also praying that David and his daughters were blessed with a memorable Christmas and that they all, including her, would hold faith that Jesus was with them and would help them, in His season as well as in all others.

David was touched by the generosity of her prayer and added his own affirmations and request that he be guided to the right space for his office and that their house become a home again.

When Jenny squeezed his hands, he knew that she understood that he was referring to much more than the repair of broken pipes.

Before they said *Amen*, he added a silent prayer for Tiffany Bower and her son Toby.

"Dad?" Rowena's voice called out. "Can we come down now?"

David opened his eyes to find Jenny studying his face in a way that made him wonder if she had experienced that unmistakable bond of praying together the way that he had.

He still wanted to seek her opinion on the office space, but he would have to do that another time because the girls had not waited for his answer and had instead found them in the parlor.

"What are you doing?" Rowena asked, but her tone wasn't accusing.

"We were praying together," David answered. He knew he wasn't always the example that he should be, but he always wanted the girls to be open to communicating to and about God.

"Like we used to with Mom?" Reba said softly. She met the eyes of her sister who, uncharacteristically quiet, nodded.

Tension threaded through him, and he couldn't help being glad that he and Jenny had dropped hands before the girls came into the room.

The truth was that, although he had tried to instill regular family prayer, Cheryl had not been a big fan of it, telling him bluntly that it was weird to hear him *all preachy and everything.* She had enjoyed the social aspect of church more than anything else.

If the girls remembered it, though, maybe it meant

more to him than he realized, and he certainly didn't want them to think that he had discredited the memory in any way.

But they both appeared curious, not upset.

"What did you pray about?" Rowena asked.

"That you have a happy Christmas," David said. "I don't think I've done the greatest job so far of making that happen."

"We're not *babies*, Dad," Rowena said. "We know there's stuff going on. We like being here, even if the decorations aren't all up. It's a cool house, and we have done some fun things."

"I guess I haven't given you enough credit for how grown-up you are both getting," David said. He briefly dashed his hand across his misty eyes and cleared his throat to hide the emotion that threatened to overwhelm him.

"We came looking for you because we made Jenny something," Reba added, and he noticed then that they both held pieces of paper.

"You made me something?" Jenny said, her voice sounding clogged with its own emotions.

They extended the papers, which turned out to be homemade cards.

"They're to say thank you for taking us shopping," Reba explained, handing the cards to Jenny who held them in her open palms like they were delicate and precious things.

David's heart did a happy dance. The problems he had were still a long way from being solved, but his daughters truly liked Jenny. He didn't know until that moment how much that meant to him.

I know things will never be what they used to be,

Lord, but I want Jenny in my life in whatever way is possible.

"Look," Rowena said, pointing. "We did colors that match our dresses. I put glitter on mine, see?"

"I see that," Jenny said, and David remembered how unabashed she could be with her emotions, just as tears began to pour down her lovely cheeks.

"Don't you like them?" Reba asked, worriedly.

Jenny nodded, laughing and crying happy tears at the same time. "I love them," she said. "I can't even tell you how much I love them!"

She opened her arms and gathered the girls in for a hug. "Thank you," she said. "I will treasure these."

David wished he could join in the hug, but it was a little too early in their tentatively healed relationship for a group-hug scenario. Instead, he clapped his hands together and asked, "Who wants sandwiches? I'll make them."

"I'll help," Jenny insisted. "You girls should still stay out of the kitchen for a little while longer."

At their request, she got down a couple of music boxes and wound them, and also retrieved an old photo album from a cabinet and encouraged the twins to try to guess which pictures were of Gran.

In the kitchen, where the smoky smell was finally abating, David and Jenny made a mini assembly line, creating sandwiches of leftover ham with Swiss cheese, lettuce and yellow mustard on grainy bread.

Occasionally, their elbows touched, and a spark of heat would rush up David's arm and tickle the back of his neck.

"Can I share a thought?" Jenny asked.

"Of course."

"I'm not a counselor, and I respect the fact that you are." She paused and took a deep breath, a sign that she was giving herself the courage to continue. "You've mentioned a few times that you want to give your daughters the perfect Christmas, and you've been blaming yourself for the obstacles that have kept that from happening and feeling guilty about it."

David opened his mouth to say something, then closed it again. She had a point.

Jenny still knew him better than anyone, he realized. Better than he wished she did.

"What I've been thinking," she continued, "is that there's no such thing as perfect. I mean there's always going to be something, or someone, that gets in the way. Maybe all *perfect* has to mean is that we're spending time with the ones we love."

She stopped talking, and the word *love* hovered between them like a beautiful, fragile ornament on a delicate Christmas branch.

Their eyes met, and like they were drawn by the same invisible magnet, they both leaned toward one another until they were a whisper's breadth apart.

"Dad," Rowe called making them both start and lean back. "Are the sandwiches ready? We're hungry."

Jenny put her hand over her mouth, and her stifled giggle stripped the last fifteen years away for a moment, except this time it was his daughters acting as chaperones instead of parents or grandparents.

David couldn't help himself: he grinned and winked at her, then called out, "Almost ready!"

"I've been telling myself the same thing," Jenny said, serious again, as they rapidly finished assembling and plating the sandwiches. "I mean about things being perfect. I guess... I guess I had this vision of coming back here, restoring this house to its former glory while being the ultimate caregiver for Gran and, somehow, still landing my dream job."

"And now?" David prodded gently, still thinking of how close his lips had come to touching hers.

"Now, I want to do what's really best for Gran, whatever that may be, and I still need to find work that pays the bills. The dream job may have to wait."

"But you did get your story in to the paper?"

Jenny nodded. "Yes, Natalie said she would use it, but she might need to make a few tweaks, which I think is pretty standard practice."

"Don't give up on your dreams, Jen," he said with an intensity that surprised them both. "I always admired you for being a dreamer and believing that the best would come. That's one of the things I always loved about you."

There was that L-word again.

He just didn't know what, if anything, he could do about it.

Chapter Thirteen

There was one thought in Jenny's head when she went to bed that night, and it was the same thought when she opened her eyes the next morning.

David and I almost kissed.

The very fact that she was thinking about it when she should be thinking about things like what the next best thing was for Gran and where she was going to find work meant that it was a large, possibly bottomless hole that she had to carefully step around.

She tried to go back to sleep but after a short fit of tossing and turning decided to make the most of the quiet house to spend time with the Lord and try to gather her thoughts.

The bedroom she was in—the one she'd always stayed in—had always been a place of safety and comfort to her. On her travels, she had felt God's presence countless times while experiencing the limitless beauty and variety of His creation. But she also always found Him here, in her grandmother's beloved home, and in some ways, though not so grand and spectacular an encounter, it was better here because He seemed closer to her heart here, more part of the fabric that wove her daily life together.

Jenny got out of bed and took a moment to smooth out and tuck in the sheets and straighten the flowered quilt that had adorned the bed for as long as she could remember.

The floor was cold beneath her feet, so she found her slippers with toes that curled upward like elves' shoes and, for good measure, pulled a sweater on over her pajama top before sitting down at the old desk, where she had done homework and written some of her best stories, and opened her Bible to Psalms.

It was really cold.

She got up again and tried to look out the window, but the glass was so frosted up she couldn't see a thing.

A tap on the door startled her.

"Gran?"

"No, it's David. I'm sorry to bother you so early..."

She went to the door and opened it. He was dressed in blue jeans and a blue-and-gray pullover sweater. His hair was appealingly tousled.

His eyes caught on her elf slippers and a flicker of amusement crossed his face before he sobered and said, "The furnace stopped running."

Dismay washed over Jenny, but then she rallied. She'd been just about to spend time with God because she loved and trusted Him. She wasn't exactly showing that if she caved in every time there was a challenge.

A broken furnace was something that could and would be fixed.

All it takes is money, which I don't have a whole lot of right now.

Last night David had praised her positivity. After they had almost kissed…

But she wasn't going to think about that.

"Who should we call?" Jenny asked. "I mean, do you know if Gran has a regular repair person she likes to use?"

David shook his head. "I have no idea," he said. "But I have someone I can call."

She was completely honest with him. "I can't afford a big bill."

"Don't worry. I'll put it on my credit card," David said. "We can sort all of that out another time."

"I can't let you do that," Jenny protested.

"Why not? Isn't that what friends are for?"

Despite the decidedly chilly house, a glow of warmth infused Jenny's spirits. Yet, she couldn't help asking, "*Are* we friends, David?"

He paused for what seemed like a long time. "Well, we're certainly not enemies." He palmed his hand over his hair. "You're not the only one who's been doing a lot of thinking, Jen. Yes, I was hurt and angry with you for many years."

Jenny tried to explain again where her head had been all those years ago, but David shook his head.

"But I've realized we were so young," he continued. "You were young, and you'd just been through one of the most challenging ordeals that anyone could go through. I understand now that you needed time to figure things out, and what kind of a Christian…what kind of a *man* would I be if I couldn't forgive you for that? Not," he added hurriedly, "that you'd done anything that needed forgiving."

"But I shouldn't have left the way I did," Jenny said, blinking back sudden tears. "I should have—"

But her words were interrupted by a plaintive cry from Gran's room. "Jenny? Are you awake, dear? Why is it so cold?"

"I'd better go to her," Jenny said, while she prayed inwardly that they would have a chance to continue their conversation. She furtively dashed the tears away with the back of her hands.

"I'll make the call," David said. "It's early, but they have twenty-four-hour emergency service."

"Which will cost even more," Jenny moaned. "And you've had all that work going on at your house."

As she said it, it hit her that the work at David's house would be done sooner or later, and then they would both get back to their normal lives—whatever that meant— and they probably wouldn't see each other, except for the inevitable running into each other from time to time.

The thought threatened to shatter her currently fragile self-control.

"I said we'll figure it out," David said.

Jenny hesitated, then nodded. Whatever the future had in store for her and David, even if it was just being able to be civil to one another, it was good not to face problems alone, for more than just financial reasons.

"Thank you," she said. "I'll pay you back, I promise."

"I know you will, but there's honestly no rush."

In Gran's room, Jenny explained that the furnace wasn't working, but that David was going to call someone to come fix it.

Gran nestled more deeply into the rose-colored comforter on her bed. Her eyes peered over the covers in a childlike manner.

"See?" she said with a sigh of contentment. "I told you that you two will always work out what to do."

The human brain was a complicated thing, Jenny mused, as she tried to adjust her face not to show her worry. How was it that Gran could remember that she'd reminded Jenny there was nothing to worry about as long as she and David were together, yet not remember that they were *not* together?

"Yes, it's nice that David is here to help out," she said carefully. "But soon he'll be going back to his own house."

And it will be me dealing with everything alone.

Which, she hurriedly assured herself, she could and would do. She had never been the type to back down from a challenge, so she wasn't going to succumb to self-doubts now, even if there were some practical things that needed to be worked out.

"His own house?" Gran repeated. "I don't know what you're talking about."

She grew fretful, fisting the quilt and scrunching her brow like an infant seeking the comfort of something or someone familiar.

"Gran, you know that—"

Just then, David appeared in the doorway.

"The furnace repairman is going to get here as soon as he can," he reported. "But it could still be a couple of hours at least. He's got another call he needs to do first."

"What should we do in the meantime, do you think?" Jenny asked. Part of her wanted to tell David about Gran's continued confusion regarding the status of their relationship, but another part thought it best not to say anything.

"I don't suppose any of the fireplaces are in working

order?" David asked, referring to the ones in the parlor and the living room.

Jenny recalled many a pleasant evening, snuggled with David, watching the fire and talking about their future.

But now she could only shake her head. "I mean, I haven't checked, but it's doubtful considering…" She let her voice trail away.

David tapped fingers on his chin, thinking.

"Okay," he said. "Well, there's no point staying here. How do you feel about going for a car ride to Yorkville?"

"Yorkville?"

"Yes," David said. "There's something I want to get your opinion on."

"I'm game," Jenny said, "as long as the car heater is working."

"Okay, I'll get the girls up, and if you can help Estelle get ready, meet you downstairs in half an hour?"

"An adventure!" Gran sat up in her bed and clapped her hands together, her bright eyes snapping with pleasure.

Jenny got out some warm clothes for Gran and then went to her own room to dress herself, all the while wondering what in the world was in Yorkville that David needed her opinion on.

But she was undeniably pleased that he did.

When they met at the front door, the twins were not nearly as pleased as Gran was at the thought of venturing out. Reba looked small and vulnerable in an oversize red sweater and old blue jeans, her face pale as she yawned hugely, making no attempt to stifle it. Rowena, also wearing jeans and the same style of sweater but in blue, was unabashedly grumpy.

"I realize this isn't ideal," Jenny said. "But I promise we'll make it fun." She wondered as she said it if she was in any position to keep that promise, but she caught David's eye, and he nodded.

"I've always liked how you do that," he said as they walked out to the car. His low, approving voice was like her favorite warm blanket. "You're always able to help people make the best of every situation."

The early morning had a hushed stillness to it, while above them stars still shone.

"I think," Jenny said, looking up, her breath making clouds in the frosty air as she spoke, "that I've had some help in making the best of things."

"Amen to that." David squeezed her gloved hand with his own, and Jenny thought that maybe Gran did know what she was talking about. It was good to have someone who understood more about the things you didn't say than the things you did.

David helped Gran and the twins into the back seat—Gran settled in between them—and he tucked a blanket around their legs. It seemed that the quiet and the starry sky had worked its wonder on Rowe and Reba too, as they were still sleepy but calm now, prepared for where the drive would take them.

Once they got going, with the heater on and the lulling motion of the moving car, the back-seat passengers soon drifted off.

"Looks like it's just you and me to carry on a conversation," Jenny said, glancing over her shoulder.

"I'm totally good with that." David kept his eyes on the road, his hands on the steering wheel, but a current of something passed between them.

"So are we going to talk about what we're not talking

about?" Jenny asked, the unusual start to the morning and the cocoon of the car making her brave.

"You mean when we almost kissed?" David asked, in his blunt way that made her smile secretly to herself because it was so familiar…and so dear to her.

"Yup, that."

He slid his eyes to her, but only briefly. He was always a conscientious driver.

I would trust him with my life.

"I'm not sure what it meant," he said, honest to a fault as he always was. "But I think that there's a part of us that will always be drawn to each other. We share so much history, after all."

She fought the urge to ask if it was only history or if there was any possibility that they had a future too?

No, it wasn't fair to ask that, and she wasn't even sure that she wanted to know. They both had plenty of their own issues to sort out.

"I don't know how I'm going to tell her," Jenny said, speaking her thoughts on one of those issues out loud.

David nodded, understanding her the way he always did. "It's not going to be easy to explain to your Gran that she might not be able to stay in her home. I can be with you if that would help any."

"I appreciate that," Jenny said. "I still can't help hoping there's an answer I haven't figured out yet."

They were silent for a moment.

"I've been praying about it," David said.

"You have?" The thought of David praying for her, on his own time, touched her on a profound level.

"Of course," he answered

Jenny's heart sped up before she reminded herself

that he would do the same for any friend, and they were friends.

And that was enough...wasn't it?

David had not been able to stop thinking about the property in Yorkville. Somehow, he knew that if he could get Jenny's reaction to it, it would help him make a decision.

His thoughts continued to jab at him about Tiffany and Toby Bower as well. Each time he had to make a decision about someone's life, it was so unbearably painful that he didn't know how he would ever do it.

Tiffany was young, and her life appeared to be jam-packed with bad choices, but that didn't mean she was a bad person at heart. But when there was a child involved, he didn't have the luxury of giving Tiffany time to prove herself. There was no sign that Toby was being abused, but there were certainly signs that he was neglected and malnourished.

"Where did you go?" Jenny's voice prodded him gently.

"Just thinking," he said, then added, "I could use your prayers too."

"Always."

He heard a promise in her voice that he had done his best to stop counting on, but now as it wound its way into his heart he wanted nothing more than to surrender to it.

The town sign for Yorkville appeared, and as he eased up on the gas preparing to enter the town, the sleepy passengers stirred.

"What are we doing in Yorkville?" Reba asked, rubbing her eyes.

"We had time for a good drive," David said, "and rumor has it that their café serves the best potato pancakes in the province."

He had never believed in bringing children into adult problems and decisions. There would be time enough to explain his decision to them if indeed he did decide to move his practice out here, and if he did decide that he would do everything he could to ensure that their lives were disrupted as little as possible.

It would help considerably that Jenny was back and that he trusted her with his girls.

Not that she was going to be his built-in sitter, he quickly amended his thoughts. But, despite his daughters' missing their mother, which was only to be expected, they liked Jenny, and they liked spending time with her. They had made it clear that they didn't want a new mother, nor was he looking to give them one.

But it was comforting, he told himself, to know that she wouldn't be far away.

"Pancakes sound good," Reba said now fully awake. She nudged Rowe, "Don't they sound good?"

"Yeah, and I'm hungry."

"We'll go soon," David promised. "How do pancakes sound to you, Estelle?"

"Anything is fine," Estelle said, in a blissful sort of way, "as long as I'm with family."

David had prepared himself for hearing Jenny's opinion no matter what it was. He had prepared himself for making a tough decision and selling that decision to his daughters.

What he had not been prepared for was the decision being made for him.

The Sold sign stared him in the face like a reminder

that, instead of trusting God, he'd already started making his own plans.

But sometimes trusting was easier said than done. was easier said than done. There was no stopping Leo from selling his current business site right out from under him, and a possible solution had just been yanked out from under his feet.

Why, then, had God led him to this property? Why had he felt so strongly that there could be answers here?

David sighed. It was probably no more than wishful thinking. He had wanted the answer to appear for him, so he let himself imagine that it had.

"What's the matter?" Jenny asked softly.

"I think this might have been a wasted trip," David murmured. "I was going to show you this building and see what you thought of it as a possibility for me to relocate my business to, but it looks like I'm too late."

"You don't know that, not for sure," Jenny said. "You could ask around and find out who bought the building. There might still be space for you there."

"Who would I ask?" David wondered.

"Didn't you say we were going for some great pancakes?" Jenny chided gently. "And haven't you learned anything living in a small town all these years? We'll just chat up whoever's at the table next to us. Someone is bound to know something."

He knew that she was half teasing, but again, with Jenny Powell around, the promise of something good to come shone brightly.

"So you think it could be a good location?" he asked.

Jenny considered for a moment, winding a strand of her hair around a finger. "I think it's not Living Skies, and I think it would be an adjustment. But... I also think there's a reason you found it."

David realized then that he hadn't told her how he had found it because he couldn't tell her what had brought him to Yorkville in the first place.

Yet, there she was, offering belief and encouragement without having to know the whole story.

That was Jenny, and it was only one of the things he had missed so much about her.

Just one of the many reasons he loved her.

Over plates of pancakes that lived up to their reputation, accompanied by crisp bacon, sausage links, a carafe of coffee for the adults and glasses of freshly squeezed orange juice for the girls, David watched Jenny effortlessly befriend not only their server but another table in her section too.

As she had predicted, the café was a great source of information.

"I heard that there's a medical clinic going in there," the server, whose name tag read Thelma said, when Jenny asked her about the property. "'Bout time too. I hear they're also looking for—whaddya call them? People you can talk to about other things that are bothering you, not just your aches and pains."

"Counselors," David said, looking right at Jenny over the coffee cup he raised to his smiling mouth.

Thelma went to get more coffee, and Jenny chewed and swallowed her last pancake bite.

"Now, that," she said with considerable satisfaction, smiling into his eyes like she used to when they were in cahoots about everything, "is what I call a God thing."

David nodded and offered up a silent prayer.

There was still much to be settled, and he had no idea how everything would play out. But for now he would simply bask in the pleasure of trusting that it would all work out.

And he would enjoy the pleasure of the company of the woman he had never really stopped missing... or loving.

Chapter Fourteen

The days edged closer to Christmas, and Jenny made the decision to postpone any kind of conversation with Gran about moving until after the big day had passed.

Being the holiday season, it wasn't likely that senior-care facilities would be doing admissions, and besides, she just wanted to be able to enjoy time with Gran doing the things they always loved to do at this time of year.

Besides, once she had the conversation with Gran, it would mean that she had to face the decision of what was going to happen with Christmas House if Gran was no longer living there.

She could easily picture herself there—it had been more her home than her parents' house had for many years—but the practicalities of living there didn't line up with her imagination.

She couldn't deny that she also woke up each morning with a thrill of anticipation in her heart at the thought of also celebrating those special moments with David and his girls.

David had found out more information on the buyers of the property in Yorkville, and it turned out that what Thelma had told them was true. Medical offices were going into that building, and they were also looking to provide counseling services.

In one of their conversations that had become habit after the others had gone to bed, David confessed to Jenny what he had previously never said out loud: he found his own practice unfulfilling, but if he joined forces with the team in Yorkville, maybe he could really start making a difference.

"You do make a difference, David," she told him, in the voice that always infused him with hope and the belief that he could face any challenge. "But if you pray about this, and your heart tells you it's time to make a change, you know I'll support you and help in any way that I can."

The days passed with David and Jenny still doing what minor repairs they could around the house and going through each room one at a time to clean them to a sparkling shine. David recruited Rowe and Reba to help too, making sure the tasks weren't too taxing for Reba, and playing holiday music as they worked.

A week before Christmas, Jenny started the day determined to speak to Fern Graham at Graham's Grocers to take Fern up on her offer of at least some temporary employment.

It wasn't her dream job, but for the time being she wasn't going to indulge in the luxury of following her heart, the way she had urged David to do. No, she would earn some money while pursuing her writing goals in her spare time.

Jenny was walking back home from a successful meeting: she would start work at the store on the first Monday after Christmas. David and the girls would very likely be back in their house by then. Her heart stuttered a little at the thought of it.

But they were friends again, who truly cared for one another, and she was so grateful for that…even if she couldn't help herself from daydreaming about more, as the unfinished kiss still lingered tantalizingly between them.

She was mentally sorting through options for Gran's care while she was working, trusting that the Lord would help her work it all out, when her phone rang.

"Hi, Jenny. Natalie here." The editor sounded brisk and a bit distracted.

"Oh, Natalie, hi. How are you?"

"I'm going to get right to the point," Natalie said, ignoring the pleasantries. "I'm not going to be able to use your story about Christmas House."

Jenny's stomach sank to her feet, even as she tried to remind herself that she was striving to trust that God had a plan.

"May I ask why?" She tried to emulate Natalie's professional tone, but the scrape in her voice indicated that she hadn't pulled it off.

"It just doesn't have that *it* factor," Natalie said. "I hate to be blunt, but it's just bit dull. I had high hopes for it, but I can't honestly say that it met my expectations."

Jenny swallowed, unsure of how to respond.

"Maybe I could try another article sometime…?"

"I can't make any promises right now. Look, I'm sorry things didn't work out," Natalie said in a voice that didn't sound all that sorry, "but writing is a tough business, and it's better to know sooner rather than later if you have what it takes. I have to get something else ready for the upcoming issue, so maybe we'll talk after the New Year."

Natalie abruptly ended the call, and Jenny was left pondering.

Something about the conversation struck her as off, apart from her bruised heart and admittedly shattered ego. Natalie had always encouraged her in the past. In fact, she could almost hear her voice back in high school praising an article Jenny had written.

But high school was a long time ago, and she really hadn't done any writing to speak of for a few years, unless she counted the journal she'd kept while traveling.

Still, disappointment gnawed like a hungry rat, and Jenny wanted most of all to sit down with David and have a good, long chat, during which he would put things back into perspective for her.

David was in the kitchen talking on his own phone when Jenny got home.

"That sounds great… Yes, yes, any time after Christmas would work well for me. I do appreciate this very much. Thanks again."

"That sounds promising," Jenny said, as he hung up and turned to her, his brown eyes lit up with anticipation.

"It is… At least, I hope it is."

"Anything you want to share?" Jenny asked, still a bit cautious. She and David had made great strides, but she didn't want to assume that she would ever again be the first person he turned to when he had news, good or bad.

But he readily said, "I've potentially taken a pretty big step. I made some calls, and after Christmas, I'm going to interview for a counseling position in York-ville."

"That's great, David," Jenny said. Her urge to vent about her own disappointing phone call from Natalie faded to a dull ache around her temples as she basked in the pleasure of being David's confidante.

"I know it's going to be a big change," David said, "and I haven't even thought about the schematics yet, with the girls and all. But I've prayed a lot about it, and I truly do feel led. I've decided to trust that things will fall into place if I get it."

"You'll get it," Jenny said. "I can't think of any rea-son in the world why you wouldn't. You have so much to offer, and you—" her cheeks pinked with sudden shyness, the pulse in her wrists pounding "—you're still the best person I know, David. You deserve ev-erything good."

David's smile slowly faded, and at first Jenny was afraid that, coming from her, the words had hit a still-tender spot. But then there was intensity in his eyes that told her that he was about as far as one could get from being offended.

He looked at her like she was something precious that he had lost and had never expected to find again.

He looked at her like he was going to—

Their lips met, and the kiss was a heady mix of fa-miliarity—the taste of his lips, the clean, soapy smell of him, the warmth of his cheek—and the appealing unfamiliarity of being kissed by the man that David had become.

But then, they both pulled back, as if mutually aware that, under their circumstances, it was not the wisest choice.

"It's just that Rowena and Reba—" the low murmur of his voice still carried the kiss "—I'm not sure what they would think. I don't want them to worry."

Jenny nodded, telling herself that it was ridiculous to be disappointed. Of course, he was right. "I understand," she said.

"But it wasn't nothing, Jen," he added firmly. "I don't kiss someone and have it mean nothing—especially not you. But before I get the girls involved, I want to make sure I understand myself what exactly we want from each other, or if we can handle wanting anything at all."

He gently cupped her face in his hands for a moment, a gesture that gentled the brisk matter-of-factness of his words.

Of all the beloved songs of the season, the most glorious one right now was her heart singing out that trust had once again been sewn between them with delicate stitches, and David was no longer shutting her out. Instead, he was opening the door for her to be a continuing part of his life.

In that moment, as she thanked God, it was easy to believe that all of their challenges would have a satisfactory answer.

If anyone had told David a few weeks ago that he would ever remember what it felt like to be young, eager and full of anticipation, he wouldn't have believed them. But, as the days sped closer to Christmas, the spring in his step and the light in his eyes were more akin to the high-school boy he had been than the burdened single father he'd become.

Simply put, everything was fun and everything seemed possible when Jenny Powell was back in his life. But the best part was that he knew he was restoring hope and confidence into her life again too.

Beyond all expectations, rising up from the fragments of his shattered dreams, the team of Hart and Powell was back, at least as friends.

They were still being cautious with the romance stuff, for a number of solid reasons, but that didn't mean that his heart didn't hiccup when her cornflower eyes captured his, or when he saw her long legs stride into the room.

There were still a number of repairs to be done at Christmas House, ones that would require the work of professional contractors. But with their combined efforts, along with Rowe and Reba, it was sparkling clean, and the living room and parlor were decorated to the hilt.

It had been a while since David had found so many reasons to thank God, but lately it seemed like the words overflowed from his heart many times a day.

One Saturday, with Christmas still a few days away, Rowena and Reba approached him, while he was at the kitchen table making notes in the Bowers' file, and Rowe taking the lead as usual said, "We're bored. Every day is like a billion hours long."

David was about to protest when he remembered that time did move differently for children especially around times like Christmas. He knew that if it wasn't for Jenny, they probably wouldn't have been in such a state of anticipation. But every day, she chatted and played with them, subtly unearthing the traditions that were meaningful to them and making sure to incorporate them into the days.

So instead of saying that life was too full of things

to do to be boring or that he was too busy, he asked, "What would you like to do?"

He closed the file with a silent prayer that Toby Bower would find a suitable and loving foster home, but even more that the little boy's mother would become the kind of person who could properly love and care for him.

"Can we go to Murphy's for lunch?" Reba asked.

When David looked at her, it hit him suddenly that she looked much less like an awkward gosling these days and more like the beautiful little girl she was. Her coloring was good, and it had been a while since she'd had any setbacks.

The Lord was being extraordinarily good to them, and his heart sang with gratitude.

"Us and Jenny and Gran too," Rowe added.

He noticed, with amusement, that they must have anticipated a *yes* because they already had ski pants on over their jeans and their hats on.

"We can go," he told them, "but I'll have to see what Jenny and her grandma are doing."

"Do I hear my name?" Jenny said as she came into the room, and he was reminded of the alertness—the sense of being more fully *alive*—that she brought out in him.

She always had, and she always would. He had just forced himself to forget that.

Her skin still looked slightly damp and flushed from a recent shower, her hair was pulled back into a ponytail, and she wore blue jeans and a pink angora sweater.

"We want to go to Murphy's for lunch," Reba told her, "and for you and Gran to come."

"Carol Barker is taking Gran to get her hair done today," Jenny said, "but I would love to join you."

The twins grinned and ran off to get their coats.

* * *

You had to be somewhat of a brave soul to face the lunch crowd at Murphy's, David often thought, especially on a Saturday so close to Christmas.

There was a line when they arrived, and the tables were filled with Living Skies's residents enjoying the best coffee in town, along with their wonderful food.

"We'll get a table soon. The line should move quickly," he reassured his daughters even as he could see that most of the diners were settled in comfortably, enjoying the reprieve from shopping.

But the girls were content, discussing what they might have for lunch.

He smiled at Jenny. "It's nice to be here with you," he said softly, meaning they were in a much better place than their first venture back to Murphy's. "I'd say kind of like old times, except..." He tilted his head subtly at his daughters.

"Better than old times," Jenny said.

David was enjoying her company, so he didn't immediately pick up on the change in the atmosphere as people became aware of their presence. Newspapers rustled, eyes shifted toward them, there were curious and oddly encouraging smiles, before attention turned back to their own conversations.

"Is there something going on here that I don't know about?" David asked Jenny in a lowered voice, trusting that she was also picking up on the peculiar vibe.

She shook her head. "Not that I know of but, yeah, everyone's acting a bit weird." She tried to pull off a chuckle, but it faltered a bit.

Then Nancy Chamberlain, their former classmate who had always been notorious for gossiping, spotted them and headed their way, clutching the Saturday newspaper in her hand.

"I had *no* idea," she gasped rather dramatically when she reached them, clutching at David's arm. "I mean, I knew your poor little girl had been sick," her eyes fell on Reba, who anxiously chewed her lower lip, while Rowena made no attempts to hide her scowl. "But I had no idea *at all* what it must be like being a single father and dealing with that kind of grief and pressure. And now Jenny's back." She gave Jenny a brief, somewhat coldly assessing look before turning her drenched-in-sympathy, seasoned-with-curiosity attention back on David. "And I'm sure *that* must carry all kinds of baggage with it too."

"What are you talking about, Nancy?" David said. "It's not exactly breaking news anymore that Reba was sick and that Cheryl left," he said. He wasn't entertaining her comment about Jenny being back. He balanced on a precarious beam of acceptance and forgiveness, and there was no way that someone like Nancy Chamberlain was pushing him off.

"Oh, I know," Nancy said as she rustled the Saturday paper a little at him. "It just didn't hit me exactly what all of it meant until I read Natalie's story."

Wordlessly, David took the newspaper from her hands, and his eyes scanned the article she pointed at.

His tentatively healed heart splintered open, his stomach dropped like he was falling in a dark dream, and the voices around him faded into the distance.

All he could see, all he could think about was Jenny and how much, how very much it hurt to realize that he couldn't trust her after all when he had so badly wanted to.

"You promised me," he said. He heard his voice grow clipped and cold. "I realize you didn't actually write the article," he said with a strange formality that was like trying to put frayed gauze over a gaping wound, "but you must have said things to Natalie that you had no right to say. You betrayed my trust...again."

"I didn't!" Jenny choked out the protest. "I didn't, David, and I wouldn't."

But in that moment, he was a seventeen-year-old boy, clutching a letter he could hardly comprehend.

And now he was a man who should have known better than to trust again.

Chapter Fifteen

Christmas Eve found Jenny at the midnight service. Making the choice to avoid David and his daughters at the earlier service caused the usually peaceful and hopeful time to be tainted, though she hoped that the familiar story of the Savior's birth and the melodies of the carols would soothe her.

Pastor Sam Meyer was preaching at the midnight service, allowing Pastor Liam and his wife to spend the time after the early service visiting family. Bill and Vivian Russell had taken Gran to the earlier service and insisted they could just as easily read and visit at Gran's house as at their own. Their offspring weren't expected until after the New Year, so it was a quiet Christmas for them.

Jenny appreciated the kindness of the Russells and others.

It didn't fix things, but it helped.

Jenny was pleasantly surprised when Grace Severight, who she hadn't seen lately other than at church on Sunday, slid into the pew beside her.

They exchanged smiles and stood in unison when the

pianist sounded the joyful opening strains of "O Come, All Ye Faithful."

Despite her best efforts to stay focused, Jenny's thoughts were in a tug-of-war between the peace and promises of the season and her undeniable anger at David Hart.

She could only imagine what he had said to the gregarious but slow-moving Bruce Willoughby to allow a return to his own home before Christmas.

She didn't even want to imagine how badly he wanted to be away from her.

Jenny had challenged David to talk to Natalie himself, and Natalie had been forthcoming—not apologetic, but at least honest—that the article had been her idea, and she had pieced it together without Jenny's knowledge or cooperation.

But it didn't matter anymore. Despite any strides they had made, it was now clear that David's fallback would be to distrust her.

They couldn't live like that. They both deserved better because, despite her anger, she loved David, and she wanted him to find happiness even if it couldn't be with her.

"Hey," Grace's whisper startled her a little. Grace elbowed her gently, her eyes filled with concern. "Relax. Whatever it is, it's going to be okay."

Jenny managed a small smile in return, realizing she couldn't hide the signs of her body's tension from the professionally trained physical therapist.

When the tears spilled down her cheeks and her chin wobbled during the singing of "Silent Night," she blamed it on the impact the carol had on many.

But it was clear that Grace didn't believe her, and

Pastor Sam's eyes lingered on her face with such kindness that Jenny almost broke down right then and there except, of course, she wouldn't even if there weren't people behind her waiting to shake the pastor's hand and wish him a Merry Christmas.

"God's got this, Jenny," Pastor Sam murmured, pressing her hand briefly between his.

Pretending she was back in high school, waiting backstage for the curtain to open, Jenny presented her most confident smile.

"Merry Christmas, Pastor Sam," she said.

There was a hush over the town, and the stars shone their glorious gratitude for their Creator as Jenny stepped outside the church.

Why can't I just admit that I hurt, God? You certainly know it, and I know we're supposed to lessen our burdens by sharing them.

But the problem with that was that the person she wanted to share her burden with, as well as all her happiest times and all the everyday moments in between, was the same person causing her burden.

God's got this. Pastor Sam's words echoed back to her. But did she really believe that? Did she herself actually trust not just God for this circumstance, for the rock of resentment that had sprung up again between her and David but for *all* of it?

Did she trust that He was with her when she'd decided to leave Living Skies and when she'd made the choice to come back? Did she trust that He was ultimately in charge of Gran's care…and of David's heart?

Did she really believe that she couldn't and didn't have to fix everything?

And, if all of that was true, where did it leave her?

She didn't know. She didn't have the slightest clue, but maybe a good place to start would be to admit that.

"Grace?" She turned back to where her friend was chatting with others. "I know it's late, but would you have time to talk?"

For a few days it seemed that God was rewarding Jenny for sharing her burden because answers began to come in ways that made her realize that solving everything never had been up to her.

For example, when she broached the subject about Gran's care, her grandmother revealed that she and Gramps had prepared for such a time. They understood and accepted the nature of their daughter and son-in-law and knew it was wise to plan for their own future care.

"But I'm not leaving this house until I see you and David settled here," Gran said. They sat in the parlor where Gran placidly nibbled on a gingersnap and sipped her tea.

Jenny sighed. "Gran?"

Gran looked up, her eyes shining like a child who believes the world to be a good place. "Yes, Jenny. What is it?"

Jenny opened her mouth then closed it again.

"Let me freshen up your tea."

She didn't want to tell Gran that she didn't know if she and David would ever mend fences again.

Besides, maybe it was time to indulge in a bit of that childlike faith herself.

After the New Year, Natalie Surasik offered Jenny a chance to write something else for the newspaper. But she seemed not fully aware of the havoc her actions had caused, and it saddened Jenny that the *Chronicle* was no longer the respected, straight-shooting newspaper it had been under Stew Wagner's watch.

So she would keep working at Graham's Grocers, and she would think and pray hard about what she wanted to write. This too would be something she would entrust into God's hands.

Because it was all about trust, she realized. Not just the trust—or lack of—that David placed in her but trust that God loved her without conditions and without end, and she didn't have to keep searching or proving herself because there were people in her life, including her own parents, whose actions had caused her to doubt her own worthiness.

Each day, she would practice what she'd learned by giving her tattered heart to God and allowing Him to help her through the days unfolding without David Hart.

And all she could do, each day, was to continue to grow as a person, while keeping her heart open in case God had plans for her and David, after all.

"Dad," Reba sat on the arm of the chair David occupied in his living room, where the surroundings reminded him each day that they didn't belong there anymore.

Rowena slid in on the other side, and they both wriggled their arms around his neck. *Being twin-teamed* he called it to himself and wondered what was on their minds.

"We are not babies, like we've told you," Rowe said in a prepared-speech kind of way.

"We pay attention, and we notice things," Reba added her line to the script, and David almost wanted to smile, except that he wasn't in much of a smiling mood these days.

He tried to focus on the good in his life. He adored

his daughters; Reba's health continued to strengthen; and although he was just getting started in his new counseling position, he already saw ways he could help people make a difference in their lives. His days were filled with challenges and surprises, including the recent application that Grace Severight had submitted to be a foster mother.

"I agree, you're not babies," David told his daughters, "and you do pay attention." He put an arm around each of them and ruffled their hair. "What's this about?"

"We think you're not happy," Rowena said.

"And you miss Jenny," Reba said.

"We miss her too," they said together.

David's sigh sent sadness down to the tips of his toes. It was true that he had escalated their return home and, in nursing his own grief, had to painfully choose to overlook their disappointment.

A choice that now seemed appallingly selfish. He couldn't fathom that he'd let his emotions get to the point that he had chosen such action. Especially when, after the initial shock of the story had worn off, he knew Jenny had had nothing to do with it.

But despite all of the counseling he gave others, he defaulted to a position of distrust, hurting those around him and hurting himself.

When was he going to stop? When was he going to stop blaming Jenny—blaming Cheryl, or anyone else for that matter—for the times that life fell short of what he wanted it to be?

The time was now. It had to be *right now*.

He kissed the top of their heads, first Reba's, then Rowe's.

"You've given me a lot to think about," he said. "Thank you."

It had taken many talks with Pastor Liam and Pastor Sam. It had taken many sleepless nights filled with sorrow-drenched prayer and deep Bible study on what it really meant to let go and forgive. It had taken daily hope-filled nudges from his daughters.

But now the three of them stood on the doorstep of Christmas House on a crisp and bright Saturday morning at the end of January. David held a huge bouquet of flowers while the twins wriggled excitedly beside him.

He breathed a prayer, squared his shoulders and rang the doorbell.

The sight of Jenny Powell in an old sweatshirt and blue jeans, face free from makeup and hair tousled in disarray was the most beautiful sight he'd ever seen.

"Jenny, please let me say what I have to say," David began.

Her blue eyes darted across the three of them. He handed her the flowers, which she took and hid her face in.

"Jenny, I am so sorry for the mistakes that I've made. I miss you, the girls and I, we all miss you…we all love you. Is there any way at all we could be part of your life?"

Jenny lifted her face. "No," she said.

David's heart careered toward a black hole, but then…

She was hugging them, flowers and all. She was crying happy Jenny tears.

"No, you can't be a *part* of my life," she said. "I want us to have a life together, all of us, for keeps."

Rowena and Reba squealed and whooped with excitement, pulling away from the embrace to run down the steps and leap about the front lawn.

"Unless, of course, you didn't mean it when you proposed to me on the swing set when we were eight, Hart," Jenny murmured, bringing her lips close to his.

"Oh, you better believe I meant it, Powell." He kissed her lightly on the lips while his daughters hooted and giggled in the background.

"I meant it then, and I mean it now, and I'll mean it forever."

He kissed her again more lingeringly and gave thanks to God for all the promises in the days to come.

Epilogue

The following Christmas

The doorbell chimed yet again, and Jenny swung the door open to greet Bill and Vivian Russell.

"Come in!" she said, beckoning them inside. "Welcome to another Christmas at Christmas House."

Rowena and Reba, wearing their respectively gold and silver sparkly new Christmas dresses, stepped forward to take their guests' coats and ushered them into where other guests gathered in the living room. Later, as the evening went on, folks would spill into the kitchen and the parlor as well.

Jenny took a moment to survey the room, her heart swelling with such gratitude that it brought happy tears to her eyes.

Christmas House was dressed from top to bottom in Christmas finery, beloved carols echoed throughout the house, and the enticing scents of peppermint, chocolate, ginger and shortbread permeated the air, with the citrusy scent of oranges mingled in, giving the sweetness a bit of levity.

She was so grateful this was her home, her home with her husband David and the wonderful girls, who were truly like daughters to her now.

She was grateful to be managing Graham's Grocers while Fern and Wilson were on a much-needed sabbatical, edging toward retirement. It gave her the opportunity to serve her friends and neighbors, and she was still able to explore her writing. Recently, a Christian publication had accepted a devotional she'd written and asked to see more.

Most of all, she was grateful for the people who filled Christmas House, bringing love into every corner. Gran was now contentedly settled into her new life in the senior-care center but always happy to visit the house she now referred to as Jenny and David's home, the way she'd always wanted.

Grace was there, using her napkin to dab a blotch of chocolate off Toby Bower's mouth. She had fought hard to foster him as a single mom, and Jenny knew that her friend's hope was to adopt him.

Rowe and Reba carried around trays of cookies, happy and proud to be playing hostesses.

And then there was David, her beloved husband, doing his best to make a positive difference in people's lives, especially his family's.

His eyes met hers, filled with a love that warmed her from head to toe.

He came to stand beside her. "Merry Christmas, Mrs. Hart. Happy?"

He put his arm around her, and she nuzzled her head onto his shoulder. Together they looked up at the angel on the Christmas tree.

Jenny rested a gentle hand on her stomach and David

laid his hand over hers. Soon, they would share with the twins and Gran the news they had found out only that morning—news of a new and precious gift.

But for now they would take time to bask in the secret they shared as both of them gave thanks to God for filling Christmas House—and their days—with family and friends, love and trust.

* * * * *

Dear Reader.

I love the Christmas season! It's a time to be with loved ones and to be grateful for all we are blessed with, not just in a material sense, but in the relationships we share with one another.

But even at Christmas, our emotions can lead us to hurt someone or be hurt ourselves. When that happens, it isn't always easy to forgive.

In this story, the hero struggles to forgive the heroine for the pain she has caused him, while she struggles with the fact that he can't move past move a long-ago grudge. Together they learn that forgiveness can open the door to beautiful new beginnings.

It is my hope that we all strive to make our relationships positive ones and learn to set aside the things that hold us back from doing that.

May the Lord hold us all in His strong and loving hands.

I appreciate you all so much and love to hear from readers at deelynn1000@hotmail.com or you can find me on Facebook, on Instagram at dlgwrites and on Twitter at dlgwrites1.

God Bless!
Donna

COMING NEXT MONTH FROM
Love Inspired

AN UNUSUAL AMISH WINTER MATCH
Indiana Amish Market • by Vannetta Chapman

With his crops failing, Amish bachelor Ethan King already has enough problems. He certainly doesn't need flighty Ada Yoder adding to his troubles. But when a family emergency requires them to work together, they'll discover that the biggest problem isn't their differences—it's their feelings for each other.

BONDING OVER THE AMISH BABY
by Pamela Desmond Wright

After a car accident, Dr. Caleb Sutter is stranded in a Texas Amish community. Then he suddenly becomes the temporary guardian to a newborn, along with pretty Amish teacher Rebecca Schroder. But the baby soon raises questions about its family history, leading Caleb to a crossroads between his past—and a future love...

THE COWBOY'S CHRISTMAS COMPROMISE
Wyoming Legacies • by Jill Kemerer

Recently divorced Dalton Cambridge can't afford to turn down a ranch manager position—even if the boss is his ex-wife's new husband's ex-wife. Besides, working for Erica Black is strictly business. But when he finds himself caring for the single mother, will he risk everything for a holiday family?

THEIR HOLIDAY SECRET
by Betsy St. Amant

Preston Green will do anything for a fake girlfriend—even bid on one at a charity auction. Lulu Boyd is the perfect choice to stop his mother's matchmaking. And it's just for one holiday family dinner. Soon it feels all too real...but another secret might make this their last Christmas together.

A COUNTRY CHRISTMAS
by Lisa Carter

Kelsey Summerfield is thrilled to plan her grandfather's upcoming wedding. But the bride's grandson, Clay McKendry, is determined to keep the city girl's ideas in check. When a series of disasters threaten to derail the big day, will they put aside their differences...and find their own happily-ever-after?

THE DOCTOR'S CHRISTMAS DILEMMA
by Danielle Thorne

Once upon a time, Ben Cooper left town to become a big-city doctor. Now he's back to run his father's clinic and spend Christmas with his daughter. Not to fall for old love McKenzie Price. But when McKenzie helps Ben reconnect with his little girl, will Ben accept this second chance at love?

LOOK FOR THESE AND OTHER LOVE INSPIRED BOOKS WHEREVER BOOKS ARE SOLD, INCLUDING MOST BOOKSTORES, SUPERMARKETS, DISCOUNT STORES AND DRUGSTORES.

LICNM0923

HARLEQUIN
PLUS

Try the best multimedia subscription service for romance readers like you!

Read, Watch and Play.

Experience the easiest way to get the romance content you crave.

Start your **FREE TRIAL** at
<u>www.harlequinplus.com/freetrial</u>.

please pardon
my cat!